BEHIND THE
BILLIONAIRE'S
GUARDED HEART

BEHIND THE BILLIONAIRE'S GUARDED HEART

BY

LEAH ASHTON

MILLS &
BOON

First published in Great Britain 2017
By Mills & Boon, an imprint of HarperCollins*Publishers*
1 London Bridge Street, London, SE1 9GF

Large Print edition 2017

© 2017 Leah Ashton

ISBN: 978-0-263-07151-1

Printed and bound in Great Britain
by CPI Antony Rowe, Chippenham, Wiltshire

For Jen—who writes beautiful messages
in cards, talks with her hands,
and giggles at all my jokes.

Thank you for all your help with this book,
and for your belief in my writing.

You're fabulous, Jen. I miss you.

PROLOGUE

THE SUNSET WAS PERFECT—all orange and purple on a backdrop of darkening blue. Just the right number of clouds stretched their tendrils artistically along the horizon.

The beach, however, was not so perfect.

It had been a warm Perth day, so April Molyneux hadn't been alone in her plans for a beachside picnic dinner. Around her, people congregated about mounds of battered fish and chips on beds of butcher's paper. Others had picnic baskets, or brown paper takeaway bags, or melting ice cream cones from the pink and white van parked above the sand dunes.

There were beach towels everywhere, body boards bouncing in the waves, children building sandcastles, women power walking along the beach in yoga pants, gossiping at a mile a minute. Then a football team jogged by, shirtless and in matching deep purple shorts.

April wanted to scream. This was *not* what she'd planned.

This was *not* a private, romantic, beachside *tête-à-tête*.

Evan lay sprawled on their picnic blanket, his back turned away from April as he scrolled through his phone.

Today was their wedding anniversary. Three years.

#anniversary #threeyears #love #romance

Right now April felt like dumping the contents of the gourmet picnic box she'd ordered all over his head—sourdough baguettes, cultured butter, artisan cheeses, muscatels and all.

'Do we *have* to do this?' Evan asked, not even looking at her.

'You mean spend time with your wife on your anniversary?' Her words were sharp, but April's throat felt tight.

The sea-breeze whipped her long blonde hair across her eyes, and she tucked it back behind her ears angrily. She sat with her legs curled beneath her, a long pale pink maxi-dress covering her platinum bikini. She stared daggers at Evan's back. His attention was still concentrated on the screen of his phone.

'You know that isn't what I meant.'

She did. But she'd spent weeks leading up to today, posting photos of their wedding to her one point two million followers.

#anniversary #threeyears #love #romance

She'd organised for the Molyneux family jet to take them up north, up past Broome. She'd found the perfect—*perfect*—private beach. She'd had the stupid picnic box couriered up from Margaret River, and she'd had her assistant organise a gorgeous rainbow mohair picnic blanket, complete with a generous donation to the Molyneux Foundation.

And then Evan had called from work as she'd been packing her overnight bag. He'd asked if they could cancel their trip. He didn't really feel like going, and could they stay home instead?

Coming to this beach had been the compromise.

It wasn't even about the beach, really. Just the photo.

All he needed to do was smile for the camera and then they could go home and eat their fancy picnic in front of the TV. Or order pizza. Whatever. It didn't matter. And Evan could eat silently, then retreat to his study and barely talk to her for the rest of the evening.

Just as he did most nights.

Again, April's throat felt tight.

Finally Evan moved. He shifted, sitting up so he could face her. He took off his sunglasses, and for some reason April did too.

For the first time in what suddenly felt like ages

he looked directly at her. Really intensely, his hazel eyes steady against her own silvery blue.

'I don't think we can do this any more,' he said. Firmly, and in a way that probably should have surprised her.

April pretended to misunderstand. 'Come on—it's just a stupid photo. We need to do this. I have contractual obligations.'

For product placement: The mohair blanket. The picnic box. Her sunglasses. Her bikini.

Donations to the Molyneux Foundation were contingent on this photograph.

Evan shook his head. 'You know what I'm talking about.'

They'd started marriage counselling only a year after their wedding. They'd stopped trying for a baby shortly afterwards, both agreeing that it was best to wait until they'd sorted things out.

But they hadn't sorted things out.

They'd both obediently attended counselling, made concerted efforts to listen to each other…but nothing had really changed.

They still loved each other, though. They'd both been clear on that.

April *knew* she still loved Evan. She'd loved him since he'd asked her to his Year Twelve ball.

To her, that had been all that mattered. Eventually

it would go back to how it had used to be between them. Surely?

'I'll always love you, April,' Evan said, in a terribly careful tone that she knew he must have practised. 'But I don't love you the way I know I should. The way I should love the woman I'm married too. You deserve better, April.'

Oh, God.

The words were all mashed together, tangled up in the salty breeze. All April could hear, repeated against her skull, was: *I don't love you...*

His lips quirked upwards. 'I guess I deserve better, too. We both deserve that love you see in the movies, or in those books you read. Don't you think? And it's never been like that for us.'

He paused, as if waiting for her to say something, but she had nothing. Absolutely nothing.

'Look, I would never cheat on you, April, but a while ago I met someone who made me think that maybe there was a bigger love out there for me, you know?' This bit definitely wasn't practised—his words were all rushed and messy. 'I respected you too much to pursue her. I cut her out of my life and I haven't been in contact with her. At all. I promise. But I can't stop thinking about her, and I...'

His gaze had long ago stopped meeting hers, but now it swung back.

He swallowed. 'I want a divorce, April,' he said with finality. 'I'm sorry.'

She could only nod. Nod and nod, over and over.

'April?'

Her throat felt as if it had completely closed over. She fumbled for her sunglasses, desperate to cover the wetness in her eyes.

'Let's just take this stupid picture,' she said, her words strangled.

His eyes widened, but he nodded.

Awkwardly, they posed—only their shoulders touching. April took the photo quickly, without any thought at all…but amazingly the beach in the photo's background was perfectly empty just for that millisecond as she pressed the button on her phone.

To her followers it would seem perfect.

A private beach, a handsome, loving husband, a glorious sunset…

Silently she cropped the image, then added her caption and hashtags.

Three amazing years with this guy! #anniversary #threeyears #love #romance

But she deleted the last hashtag before she posted it:

#over

* * *

Hugh Bennell's gaze was drawn to the black door at the top of the grey stone stairs. The paintwork and brass door hardware all looked a bit dull—and not just because the sun was only just now rising on this rather dreary London morning. A handful of leaves had gathered where a doormat should be, and a single hopeful weed reached out from beneath the doorstep.

He'd have to sort that out.

But for now he simply wheeled his bike—lights still flashing from his pre-dawn ride—straight past the steps that led to the three-storey chocolate and cream Victorian end-of-terrace, and instead negotiated a matching set of steps that led downwards to his basement flat.

Inside, the cleats on the base of his cycling shoes clicked on the parquet flooring, and his road bike's wheels squeaked noisily. He hung the bike on its wall hanger, immediately across from the basement front door. Above it hung his mountain bike, and to the right of that was the door to one of his spare bedrooms.

That door was painted white, and the paintwork still gleamed as fresh as the day he'd had the apartment painted. He noted that the brass knob still shone—in fact his whole house shone with meticulous cleanliness, just as he liked it.

Hugh settled in at his desk after a shower, his dark hair still damp. The desk was right at the front of his apartment, pushed up against the window. Above him foot traffic was increasing as London got ready for the workday. From his viewpoint all he could see were ankles and feet—in heels and boots and lace-up shoes. The angle was too acute for anyone passing to see him—he'd checked, of course—so he could leave his blinds open, allowing natural light to filter across his workspace.

He placed his mug of tea on the coaster immediately to the right of his open laptop. Beneath that lay the day's to-do list, carefully formulated and hand-written the previous evening.

He'd always loved lists, even as a young kid. He remembered his mum's bemusement when he'd stuck a list above his bedside table to remind himself what to pack for school each day of the week. He'd found it calming to have it all written out—a much better alternative, he'd thought, to his mother's panicked realisations at the school gate and her frantic delivery of forgotten sports shoes at morning break.

'A neat freak with lists!' His mum had laughed. *'How could you possibly be mine?'*

To the bottom of his list for today he added *Paint front door and polish brass.*

He was certain the team at Precise thought his

penchant for paper lists eccentric for a man who owned and ran a multi-million-dollar mobile app empire—but then, the team thought him eccentric for many more reasons than that.

A reminder popped up on his screen for a nine a.m. appointment, and he clicked through to sign in for the online meeting. Already four of the five other attendees were logged in, their faces visible via their webcams in a grid to the right of screen.

But in Hugh's box there was only the generic grey silhouette—he never chose the video option, and he kept the camera at the top of his laptop taped over just in case.

Because, for Hugh Bennell, maintaining his privacy was non-negotiable.

He was in control of exactly what he revealed to the world.

His laptop dinged as the final attendee arrived.

'Looks like everyone's here,' Hugh said. 'Let's get started.'

CHAPTER ONE

Six weeks later—London

APRIL FELT GOOD.

She was thirty-two, and her first ever job interview was today.

Sure, she'd been interviewed for the couple of internships she'd had back at uni, but they didn't count. Today was her first real-life *I actually really, really want this job* interview.

That was significant.

She smiled.

Around her, the Tube train was packed. Everyone looked completely absorbed in their own world— reading a book, swiping through a phone, gazing out of the window into the blackness of the tunnel.

Nobody noticed her. Nobody realised how momentous this day actually was.

Since her disastrous wedding anniversary there'd been weeks of numbness for April. There'd been shock, then anger, then the awfulness of telling her mum and her sisters, Ivy and Mila. There'd been weeks of meetings with lawyers and endless discussions about property settlement. There'd been tears and wine and long conversations.

Time had seemed to go on and on. Especially at night, when she'd been alone in her ridiculously too big concrete-and-angles home. Mila had stayed a few nights to keep her company—but she had her own life and a partner to worry about. Her mum had stayed every night for a fortnight, determinedly focusing on the practicalities of lawyers and legal details. Ivy had brought her son, Nate, to visit regularly—although she had been mortified when the toddler had accidentally pushed a salad bowl off the table, shattering it into millions of pieces.

'Don't worry about it,' April had reassured her. 'It's one less thing we need to decide who gets to keep.'

At first, sorting out the things that she and Evan had bought together had seemed vitally important. Maybe it was the focus it had given her—or maybe there was more of her ruthless businesswoman mother in her than she'd thought.

But as the weeks had worn on, and she'd spent more time staring at her ceiling, not sleeping, all their *stuff* had begun to feel meaningless.

As it probably should for a woman with a billion-dollar family trust that she held with her sisters.

So Evan could have everything. Of course he could have everything.

I don't love you...

April didn't sugar-coat what Evan had said. He'd wrapped it up in superfluous words to blunt the blow, but that didn't hide the reality: Evan didn't love her. He'd never loved her—at least not the way April had loved him.

In those endless nights she'd analysed that relentlessly.

How could she not have known?

I don't love you.

You.

Who was she, if not married to Evan?

The feminist within her was horrified that she could even ask herself this question. But she did. Again and again:

Who was she?

This woman Evan hadn't loved enough. This woman who had been oblivious to the end of her marriage.

Who was she?

She was thirty-two, single and had never worked a day in her life.

Her home had been a wedding gift from her mother.

Everything she'd ever bought had been with a credit card linked to the Molyneux Trust. She had been indulged by a family who probably didn't think her capable of being anything but a frivolous socialite. Why would they? She'd applied herself to nothing else. Her days had been filled with shopping and expensive charity luncheons. Her evenings with art gallery openings and luxurious fundraising auctions. She'd spent her spare time taking photos of herself and posting them online, so millions of people could click '*like*' and comment on her fabulous perfect life.

What a sham. What a joke.

She hadn't earned a cent of the fortune she'd flouted to the world.

And her husband hadn't loved her.

She was a fraud.

But no more.

April smoothed the charcoal fabric of her pencil skirt over her thighs. It wasn't designer. In fact it had probably cost about five per cent of the cost of her favourite leather tote bag—which she'd left back home in Perth.

She'd left everything behind.

She'd booked a one-way ticket to London and opened up a new credit card account at her bank—politely declining the option to have the balance cleared monthly by the Molyneux Trust. From now on she was definitely paying her own way.

She'd also located her British passport—a document she had thanks to her mother's dual citizenship of both Australia and the UK.

Only then had she told her family what she was doing.

And then she'd ignored every single one of their concerns and hopped onto her flight the next day.

Now here she was. Three days in London.

She'd found a flat. She'd bought reasonably priced clothes for the first time in her life. She'd researched the heck out of the environmental sustainability consulting firm where she was about to have an interview.

Oh—as she noted her long ponytail cascading over the shoulder of her hound's-tooth coat—she'd also dyed her hair brown.

She felt like a different person. Like a *new* person.

She even had a new name, of sorts.

The name that was on her birth certificate and her passport: April Spencer.

Like her sisters, she'd made the choice to use her mother's surname within a few years of her father leaving them. But she'd never bothered having it formally changed.

Turned out that had now come in handy.

Today she didn't feel like April Molyneux, the billionaire mining heiress whose life had collapsed around her.

Today she was April Spencer, and today she had a job interview.

And for the first time in six weeks she felt good.

* * *

As Hugh probably should've expected, it had rained through the remainder of September and then most of October. So it was a cool but clear November morning when he retrieved the tin of black paint from beneath his stairs and headed out from his basement to the front door of the main house.

It was just before sunrise, and even on a work-day Islington street was almost deserted. A couple walking a Labrador passed by as he laid out his drop cloth, and as he painted the occasional jogger, walker or cyclist zipped past—along with the gradually thickening traffic.

It didn't take long to paint the door: just a quick sand-down, a few minor imperfections in the wood-work to repair, then a fresh coat of paint.

Now it just needed to dry.

The door had to stay propped open for a few hours before he could safely close it again. He'd known this, so he'd planned ahead and dumped his back-pack—which contained his laptop—in the hallway before he'd started work. Now he stepped inside, his work boots loud on the blue, cream and grey geometric tessellated tile entryway.

He yanked off his boots, grabbed his laptop out of his bag and then on thick socks padded over to the grand staircase ahead of him. To his left was the first of two reception rooms on the ground floor—but he wasn't going to work in there. Instead he settled on a stair third from the bottom, rested his laptop on his jeans and got to work.

Or at least that was the plan.

Instead his emails remained unread, and the soft beep of instant message notifications persisted but were ignored.

Who was he kidding? He was never going to get any work done in here.

It was impossible when his attention remained on insignificant details: the way the weak morning sunlight sauntered through the wedged-open door to mingle with the dust he'd disturbed. The scent of the house: cardboard packing boxes, musty air and windows closed for far too long. The light—or lack of it. With every door but the front door sealed shut, an entryway he remembered as bright with light seemed instead gloomy and...*abandoned*.

Which, of course, it was.

He hadn't stepped foot in here since the day he'd moved into the basement.

Back then—three years ago—it had been too hard. He hadn't been ready to deal with this house.

Hugh stood up, suddenly needing to move. But not out through the front door.

Instead he went to the internal door only a few steps away and with a firm grip twisted the brass knob and yanked the door open.

He hadn't realised he'd been holding his breath—but he let it out now in a defeated sigh. As if he'd expected to see something different.

But he'd known what was in here.

Once, this room had been where his mother and her second husband had hosted their guests with cups of tea and fancy biscuits.

That would be impossible now. If any antique furniture remained, it was hidden. Completely. By boxes. Boxes that filled the room in every direction—stacked neatly like bricks as tall as he was—six foot and higher.

Boxes, boxes, boxes—so many he couldn't even begin to count.

Hugh reached out to touch the nearest box. It sat on a stack four high, its plain cardboard surface slightly misshapen by whatever was crammed within it.

Some of the many boxes that surrounded it—beneath, beside and beyond—were occasionally labelled unhelpfully: *purple treasures…sparkly things*.

Others—the work of the woman Hugh had employed to help his mother—had detailed labels and colour-coded stickers: a relic of Hugh's attempts to organise his mother's hoard into some sort of system.

But his mother had resisted—joyfully creating ridiculous categories and covertly shuffling items between boxes—and in the end her frustrated assistant had correctly informed Hugh that it was an utter waste of time.

Which he'd already known—but then, what option had he had?

Doctors, specialists, consultants…all had achieved nothing.

How could they? When his mother knew exactly what she was doing?

She'd been here before, after all. Before Len. When it had been just Hugh and his mum and her hoard. And her endless quest for love.

With Len she'd finally had the love she'd searched for for so long. A love that had been powerful enough to allow her to let go of all the things she'd collected in the years since Hugh's father had left them. Things she'd surrounded herself with and held on to so tightly when she'd been unable to possess the one thing she'd so badly wanted: love.

Without Len his mother had believed that her hoard was all she'd had left. And, despite still having Hugh, despite his desperate efforts, it hadn't been enough.

He'd been helpless to prevent the hoard that had overshadowed his childhood from returning.

Hugh closed his eyes.

There was so much *stuff* in this room that if he walked another step he would walk into a wall of boxes.

It was exactly the same in almost every room in the house—every living space, every bedroom. Except the kitchen, halls and bathrooms—and that was only because of the staff Hugh had employed and his mother's reluctant agreement to allow them into the house each day.

So that was all he'd managed: to pay people to keep the few bits of empty floor space in his mother's house clean. And to clear a safe path from her bedroom to the front and back doors in case of a fire.

Really, it was not all that different from how it had been when he'd been ten. Except this time he'd had loads of money to outsource what he'd only barely managed as a kid.

And this place was a hell of a lot bigger than the tiny council flat he'd grown up in.

He opened his eyes, but just couldn't stare at those awful uniform boxes any more.

Back in the entry hall, Hugh grabbed his laptop and backpack, ready to leave…but then he stilled.

The new paint on the door was still wet. He wasn't going anywhere.

But he also wasn't going to be able to work—it would seem that three years had done nothing to ease the tension, the frustration and the hopelessness that those damn boxes elicited within him.

Even waiting another three years—or ten—to deal with them wasn't going to make any difference.

They'd still represent a lot more than they should. They needed to go. *All* of them.

This house needed to be bright and light once again. It needed to breathe.

So he sat back down on the bottom step of the grand old staircase, knowing exactly what he was going to do.

It was time.

It had started with confusion at the supermarket checkout.

'Do you have another card?' the checkout operator had asked.

'Pardon me?' April had said—because, well, it had never happened to her before.

It had, it seemed, happened several times to the not particularly patient operator—Bridget, according to her name tag. She'd studied April, her gaze flat, as April had tried what she knew to be her correct PIN twice more.

And then, as April had searched hopelessly for an alternative card—she'd cut up every single card linked to the Molyneux Trust back in Perth—Bridget had asked her to move aside so she could serve the next in a long line of customers.

April had dithered momentarily: was she supposed to return the Thai green curry ready-meal, the bunch of bananas and bottle of eye make-up remover to the shelves before she left?

But then the weight of pitying stares—possibly only imagined—had kicked in, and April had exited the shop as fast as she'd been able, her sneakers suddenly unbelievably squeaky on the supermarket's vinyl flooring.

Now she was at home, still in her gym gear, on her butter-soft grey leather couch, her laptop before her.

For only the second time in the four weeks since she'd been in London she logged in to her internet banking—the other time being when she'd set up her account at the bank. Her fully furnished flat didn't come with a printer, so she'd have to scroll through her credit card statement onscreen.

But it was still easy to see the reason for her mortification at the checkout—she'd maxed out her credit card.

How was that even *possible*?

She'd been so careful with her spending—more so as each still jobless week had passed.

She hadn't bought any new clothes for *weeks*. She'd stopped eating at cafés and restaurants, and had instead become quite enamoured with what she considered a very English thing: convenience stores with huge walls of pre-made sandwiches in triangular plastic packaging. And microwaveable ready-meals for dinner.

They must only be costing a few pounds a meal, surely?

She *had* joined the gym, but that had seemed very cheap. And fortunately the flat came with Wi-Fi, so she hadn't had to pay for that.

So where had all her money gone?

Five minutes later she knew.

With pen and paper, she'd documented exactly where her money had been spent.

Her rent—and four weeks' deposit—was the biggest culprit. Only now did it dawn on her that even if she *did* get one of the many, many jobs she'd been applying for, her starting salary would barely cover her rent. With absolutely nothing left over for sandwiches in plastic triangles.

She flopped back onto her couch and looked around her flat.

It was small, but—if she was objective—not *that* small. And it was beautifully furnished. *Expensively* furnished. Her kitchen appliances were the same insanely priced brand she'd had back in Perth. Her small bathroom was tiled in floor-to-ceiling marble.

She even had a balcony.

But she couldn't afford a balcony. She couldn't afford any of this.

Because she didn't have any money. *At all*.

Not for the first time in four weeks, she wondered if she'd made a terrible mistake.

The first time had been after she hadn't got the first job she'd been interviewed for.

Now, several job interviews later—and many more applications that had led to absolutely nothing—her initial optimism astounded her. She literally had a degree, an internship and then almost ten years of nothing.

Well—not *nothing*. But nothing she was about to put on her CV. A million followers and a charitable foundation that she'd established herself could possibly sound impressive to *some* HR departments. But they weren't relevant to the environmental officer roles she was applying for.

And, just as importantly, they would reveal her real name. And she just couldn't do that.

Although it was tempting at times. Like tonight. How easy it would be to still be April Molyneux and organise the reissue of one of the many credit cards linked to her insane fortune? By this time tomorrow she could be eating all the Thai green curry she wanted.

She could even upgrade to a far more impressive flat.

April pushed herself up and off the couch, to search for something to eat in her lovely kitchen.

Her fridge was stocked only with expensive Australian Riesling, sparkling designer water— also expensive—a partially eaten wheel of camembert cheese—expensive—and the organic un-homogenised milk that she'd bought because she'd liked the pretty glass bottle it came in— probably also more expensive than it needed to be.

April felt sick.

Was she really so disconnected from the reality of what things cost?

Her whole life she'd known she was rich. But she'd thought she still had *some* sense of the reality of living in the real world: without a trust fund, without the mansion your mum had bought for you.

She'd liked to think she'd projected some sort of 'everywoman' persona to her Instagram and Facebook followers. That despite the good fortune of her birth that she was really just like everybody else.

She poured herself a bowl of probably overpriced granola and used up the rest of her fancy milk, then sat back in front of her laptop.

Earlier today, before heading to the gym, she'd scheduled the next couple of days' worth of social media posts.

April *Spencer* might be in London, but April Molyneux—to her followers, anyway—was still in Perth, effortlessly adjusting to her new single life.

Before she'd dyed her hair she'd made sure she'd honoured every single product placement agreement she'd signed, and had posed for months' worth of photos. She'd taken even more selfies, with all manner of random backgrounds—she'd come up with something to caption them with as she needed to.

Plus she still took random photos while here in London—the habit was too ingrained for her to give it up completely. She just made sure her hair and anything identifiably London wasn't in any of the photos. So the book she was reading...the shade she'd painted her toenails...that kind of stuff. All was still documented, still shared, interwoven with her blonde April photos and carefully coordinated with her assistant back home—thankfully still paid for by the Molyneux Foundation.

So her social media life carried on. Her followers continued to grow.

And what were they seeing?

She scrolled down the page, taking in her last few years of photos in a colourful blur.

A blur of international holidays, secluded luxury Outback retreats, designer shoes, amazing jewellery, beautiful clothes, a gorgeous husband and attractive—wealthy—friends.

They were seeing an unbelievably privileged woman who had absolutely no idea what it was like to exist in the real world.

April slapped her laptop screen shut, suddenly disgusted with herself.

And ashamed.

The whole point of all this—the move to London,

her quest for a job, living alone for the first time in her life—had been about finding herself. Defining who she was if she wasn't Evan's wife. Or one of the Molyneux heiresses.

But so far all she'd achieved was a self-indulgent month during which she'd patted herself on the back for 'living like a normal person' but achieved absolutely nothing other than a new, reasonably priced wardrobe.

She knew her mum, Ivy and Mila all assumed this was just a bit of a game to her. They assumed that once she did eventually get a job she'd supplement her income with Molyneux money. On reflection, no one had pointed out the now damned obvious fact that she couldn't afford this apartment.

And, unlike April, they would know. Mila had never used her Molyneux fortune: she knew exactly how far a dollar or a pound could stretch. And Ivy had dedicated her life to building up the Molyneux fortune—so she knew, too.

She couldn't even be annoyed with them. Up until tonight, and that stupid, sad 'declined' beep at the cash register, they'd been right.

They'd been right to think that their pampered middle sister couldn't cut it in the real world.

And, if she was brutally honest, she hadn't even been trying. She'd *thought* she had, but people in the real world didn't have no income for a month—

and no savings—and then casually take their time applying for some mythical perfect job while living in a luxury apartment.

She flipped her laptop open again.

She needed to find a job. Immediately.

CHAPTER TWO

SHE HAD A nice voice, Hugh thought.

Unquestionably Australian. Warm. Professional.

She didn't sound nervous, although she did laugh every now and again—which was possibly nerves. Or possibly not. Her laugh was natural. Also warm. Pretty.

Hugh's lips quirked. How whimsical of him. How unlike him.

Currently, April…he glanced down at the printed CV before him…April *Spencer* was answering the last of his four interview questions.

Rather well, actually.

He leant back in his chair, listening carefully as her voice filled the room, projected by the speakers hooked up to his laptop.

This was the third interview his recruitment consultant had organised, although the other two applicants had been quite different from April. One an art curator, another an antique specialist.

Both complete overkill for the position. He'd been clear with the consultant, Caro, that his mother's collections were not of any monetary value—although Caro *had* made some valid points that knowledge of antiques and curation skills might still be of use.

But still… He felt as if employing either skill-set would be pretending that all those boxes were something more than they actually were. Which was a hoard. A hoard he wanted out of his life.

'…so I feel my experience working for the Molyneux Foundation demonstrates my understanding of the importance of client privacy,' April said as she continued her answer. 'I regularly dealt with donors who requested their names remain absolutely confidential. At other times donors wished for their donation—whether it be product, service or otherwise—to be announced at a date or time suitable to their company. In both scenarios complete discretion was essential.'

'But your role at the foundation, Ms Spencer, was as social media coordinator,' Hugh prompted, scanning her CV. 'Why would you have access to such sensitive information?'

There was the briefest pause. 'It's quite a small foundation,' April said, her tone confident. 'And I worked closely with the managing director. It was my job to schedule posts and monitor comments— I needed to know what to announce, and also what comments to remove in case anyone gave one of our generous benefactors away.'

From the notes Caro had provided, it seemed April's work with the Molyneux Foundation had been the reason she'd been put forward. Hugh had made it clear that a proven ability to maintain strict confidentiality was essential for this position.

'And you're available immediately?' he asked.

'Yes,' April said.

Hugh nodded at the phone. 'Right—thank you, Ms Spencer,' he said. 'A decision will be made shortly.'

Then he ended the call.

After the interview April left the small meeting room and returned to the recruiter's office.

It had all been rather bizarre. She'd come in this morning expecting to be assigned to an interview for something similar to her two jobs so far—both short-term entry level social media roles to cover unexpected leave—and yet she'd been put forward for a job unpacking boxes, with a phone interview to take place almost immediately.

Across from her, at her large, impressive desk, sat Caroline Zhu, the senior recruiter at the agency April had been working for since her supermarket debacle three weeks earlier.

'I'm sorry,' April said. 'I don't think the interview went particularly well.'

Terribly, actually. She felt she'd answered the questions well enough, but Hugh Bennell had barely said a word. Certainly not a word of encouragement, anyway.

'Possibly,' Caro said, in the no-nonsense voice that matched her jet-black no-nonsense ponytail. 'But unlikely. It's been several years since Mr Bennell has required my services, but I'm certain his interview technique has not changed. He is not one for superfluous conversation.'

April nodded. Yes, she'd got that.

It fitted, she supposed—her frantic internet searching in the short period of time she'd had before her interview had revealed little about Hugh Bennell. She knew of Precise, of course—practically everyone with a smartphone would have at least one app from the company. April, in fact, had about six, all related to scheduling, analytics and online collaboration. But, unlike other international tech companies that were synonymous with their founders, Hugh Bennell was no more than a name on the company website—and the subject of several newspaper articles in which a string of journalists had attempted to discover the man behind such a massive self-made fortune.

But all had failed.

All April had learnt from those quickly skimmed articles was that Hugh had grown up in council housing in London, the only child of a single, hardworking mother. As soon as he'd left university it had been as if he'd wiped all trace of himself from public record—she'd found no photos of him, and his Wikipedia entry was incredibly brief.

It was strikingly unusual in this share-everything world.

Mysterious, even.

Intriguing, actually.

'You'll know soon enough,' Caroline continued. 'In my experience, Mr Bennell makes extremely swift decisions.'

'Are you able to tell me a bit more about the position?'

Caroline raised an impatient eyebrow. 'As I said, the information Mr Bennell provided is limited. He has a room full of a large number of boxes that require sorting and disposal. Not antiques. Nothing dangerous. He requires someone trustworthy and hardworking who can start immediately. That's all I can tell you.'

'And you thought I was suitable because...?'

'Because you're keen to work as much as possible for as much pay as possible. You were quite clear on that when we first met.'

True. After some judicious reimagining of her work experience—she'd repositioned herself as April Spencer, Social Media Manager at the Molyneux Foundation, which was technically true—she'd turned up at the best-reviewed temp agency within walking distance of her overpriced flat at nine a.m. the Monday after her credit card had been declined.

She'd been absolutely—possibly over-zealously— clear in her goals. To work hard and earn as much money as she could. In fact, she'd even found a night job, stacking shelves at a supermarket near her new home.

She needed her credit card debt cleared *pronto*. She needed money *yesterday*.

Fortunately Caroline Zhu had seemed to consider her desperation-tinged enthusiasm a positive.

The phone rang in pretty musical tones.

'Ah, here we go,' Caroline said, raising her eyebrows at April. She picked up the phone, had the briefest of conversations that ended with, 'Excellent news, Mr Bennell. I'll let the successful applicant know.'

She hung up and turned back to April.

'Just as I thought,' Caroline said. 'I'm rarely wrong on such things. Mr Bennell has selected you as his preferred candidate. You start immediately.'

'Unpacking boxes?'

'For a mouthwatering sum an hour.'

'I'm in,' April said with a grin.

Caroline might have let slip the slightest of smiles. 'You already are. Here's the address.'

* * *

Hugh Bennell's house was beautiful.

It felt familiar, actually—she'd stayed with her mum and sisters at a similar house for Christmas, many years ago. It was the year she and her sisters had campaigned for a white Christmas and, like so many things in her childhood and adult life, it had just happened.

She straightened her shoulders, then knocked on the front door.

She'd been told Hugh Bennell would be meeting her—which had surprised her. Surely the boss of a company like Precise had staff to deal with a lowly employee like herself?

But then, she'd supposed he also had staff to *interview* lowly employees like herself—and he'd already done that himself.

If anything, it just added to the general sense of mystery: mysterious boxes for her to unpack, complete with a mysterious billionaire CEO who was mysteriously hands-on with the recruitment of unskilled labour.

It was late morning now. She hadn't had time to change, so she still wore what she now considered her 'interview suit'. Her shoes were freshly polished, and her hair was looped in an elegant low bun that she was rather proud of. Her stylist back in Perth would be impressed.

The liquorice-black door opened.

And revealed a man.

A tall man. With dark hair, dark stubble. Dark eyes.

Dark eyes that met her own directly. *Very* directly.

Momentarily April felt frozen beneath that gaze.

So this is what a mysterious tech billionaire looks like.

Jaw-droppingly handsome.

She blinked. 'Good morning,' she said, well practised from years of socialising at every event anyone could imagine. 'I'm April Spencer. Are you Mr Bennell?'

He nodded. 'You got here quickly.'

'I did,' she said. 'The agency emphasised the urgency of this placement.'

Silence. But, despite her usually sparkling conversational skills, April didn't rush to fill it. Instead she simply stood still beneath Hugh Bennell's gaze.

He was still looking at her. Unreadably but intensely. It was a strange and unfamiliar sensation.

But not entirely uncomfortable.

There was something about him—the way he stood, maybe—that created a sense of calm. And of time.

Time to take a handful of moments to study the man before her—to take in the contrast of his black hair and olive skin. To admire the thick slashes of his eyebrows, the sharpness of his cheekbones, the elegance of his mouth.

He was more interesting than gorgeous, she realised, with a slightly crooked nose and an angular chin. His too-long hair and his stubble—forgotten, she was sure, rather than fashionable.

But it was that sum of those imperfect parts that made a darkly, devastatingly attractive whole.

And definitely not what she'd been expecting.

Whatever she'd thought a mysterious billionaire who deliberately shunned the spotlight would look like, *this* was not it.

He was also *nothing* like Evan.

That realisation came from left field, shocking her.

April blinked again. *What was she doing?*

'Please come in,' Hugh Bennell said. As naturally as if only a beat of time had passed.

Maybe it had?

April felt flustered and confused—and seriously annoyed with herself.

She'd just met her new boss. She needed to pull herself together.

She was probably just tired from the long hours she'd been working.

But did tiredness explain the way her gaze documented the breadth of her new boss's shoulders as she stepped inside?

Nope.

There was no way she could pretend she didn't know what the fireworks in her belly meant. It had just been a *long* time since they'd been associated with anyone but her husband.

And a pretty long time since she'd associated them with Evan.

She squeezed her eyes shut for a second.

No. No. No, no, *no.*

She had not flown halfway around the world to turn into a puddle over a man. Over her *boss*. No matter how mysterious.

That certainly wasn't why she was working two jobs and sharing a room in a truly awful shared house.

She'd come to London to live independently. Without her mother's money for the first time in her life and without Evan for the first time since she was seventeen.

And she needed this job. She certainly needed the very generous hourly rate.

She *didn't* need fireworks, or the heat that had pooled in her belly.

'Miss Spencer?'

April's eyes snapped open. 'Sorry, Mr Bennell.'

'Are you okay?' he asked.

He did have gorgeous eyes. Thoughtful eyes that looked as if a million things were happening within them.

'Of course,' she said with a deliberate smile.

He inclined his chin, somewhat sceptically. 'I was just saying that we'll run through your responsibilities in the kitchen.'

She nodded, then followed him down the narrow hall beside the rather grand if dusty staircase.

As they walked April did her absolute best to shove all thoughts of fireworks or heat firmly out of her mind—and her body. Frustratingly, Hugh's well-worn, perfectly fitted jeans did nothing to help this endeavour.

Neither did the unwanted realisation that—for the first time since Evan had told her he didn't love her and her sparkling life had been dulled—she felt truly alive.

April Spencer was beautiful.

Objectively beautiful. As if she'd stepped off the pages of a catalogue and into his mother's house.

For a while he'd stood and just *looked* at her, because he'd felt helpless to do anything but.

He'd looked at her chocolate-brown hair, at her porcelain skin and her crystal blue eyes. At her lips—pink, and shining with something glossy. At her fitted clothes and the long coat cinched in tight at her waist.

He'd expected a backpacker. Someone younger, really. Someone he could actually imagine lifting and shifting boxes.

This woman was not it.

This woman was poised and utterly together. Everything about her exuded strength and confidence. As if she was used to commanding a room. Or a corporation.

Not rummaging through boxes.

It just didn't fit.

He'd let her in, but then he had turned to face her—to question her.

He needed to know who she was and what she was doing here.

But when he'd turned her eyes had been closed.

He'd watched her for a second as she'd taken deep breaths. In through her nose. Out through her mouth. And it was in that moment—while that knowledgeable gaze had been hidden—that he'd sensed vulnerability. A vulnerability that had been completely disguised by her polish and her smile.

And so, instead of interrogating her, he'd asked her if she was okay.

And instead of calling the agency back, asking for someone more suitable, he'd led her into the kitchen and handed her a confidentiality agreement to sign.

That moment of vulnerability had long gone now, and the woman in his mother's kitchen revealed nothing of whatever he'd seen.

But he *had* seen it. And he of all people knew that people were rarely what they first appeared. He'd spent most his life hiding all but what people absolutely needed to know.

So for now he wasn't going to question April Spencer.

But he *did* acknowledge her incongruity, and he didn't like that this project to clear his mother's house already felt more complicated than he wanted it to.

April laid his pen on top of the signed paperwork. 'All done, Mr Bennell,' she said with a smile.

'Call me Hugh,' he said firmly.

'April,' she said, with eyes that sparkled.

He was again struck by her beauty, but forced himself to disregard it. The attractiveness of his employees was none of his concern.

He nodded briskly, and didn't return her smile. 'You'll be working alone,' he said, getting straight to the point, 'and I've provided guidelines for how I want items sorted. It should be self-explanatory: paperwork containing personal details is to be saved, all other papers to be shredded and recycled. Junk is to be disposed of. Anything of value should be separated for donation. I've provided the details of local charities you can contact to organise collection.'

April nodded, her gaze on the printed notes he'd left for her.

'Is there anything other than papers you want kept?' she asked.

'No,' he said.

Maybe louder than he'd intended, as her head jerked upwards.

'Okay,' she said carefully. 'And how do I contact you if I have any questions?'

'You don't,' he said. 'I'm not to be disturbed.'

Her glossy lips formed a straight line. 'So who *can* I contact?'

He shrugged dismissively. 'You won't need to contact anybody. It's all made very clear in my instructions. Just send me an email at the end of each day with details of your progress.'

'So you *know* what's in the boxes? Caroline implied that you didn't, which is why you need me to sort through them.'

Hugh shook his head. 'It doesn't matter.'

April met his gaze. 'So you trust me to go through a whole room of boxes and make all the decisions myself?'

'Yes,' he said. 'It's all junk. You aren't going to stumble across a hidden fortune, I promise you.'

She looked unconvinced.

'And besides—it's not a room. It's the whole house.'

Her eyes widened. 'Pardon me?'

He ran a hand through his hair. He just wanted this conversation to be over and to be out of this place. This stuffed full, oppressive house which this woman only complicated further.

'Yes,' he said. 'Three floors. Leave any furniture where it is. Don't lift anything too heavy. I've left you a key and the security code. I expect you to work an eight-hour day.' He stopped, mentally running through any further extraneous details he should mention. 'If there's an emergency—*only* an emergency—you can call me. My number is listed in the documentation.'

'That's it?' she said.

'That's it,' he said.

'Great,' she said. 'Where do I start?'

'I'll show you,' he said.

Minutes later they stood before a wall built with pale brown cardboard.

'Wow,' April said. 'I've never seen anything like this before.'

Hugh had.

'Did you buy the place like this?' she asked.

'Something like that,' he said, needing to leave. Not wanting to explain.

She'd work it out soon enough.

'I'll get this sorted for you,' April said, catching his gaze.

He already had one foot in the foyer.

She spoke with assurance—*reassurance?*—and with questions in her eyes.

But Hugh didn't want to be reassured, and he certainly didn't want her questions. He hated the way this woman, this stranger—*his employee*—thought he needed to be somehow comforted.

He'd barely said a word since they'd entered this room—what had he revealed?

'That's what you're here for,' he said firmly.

Nothing more.

Now he could finally escape from the boxes, and his breath came steadily again only as he closed the front door behind him.

CHAPTER THREE

TWO DAYS LATER April sat cross-legged amongst a lot of boxes and a lot of dust.

She was dressed in jeans, sneakers and a floppy T-shirt—her jumper having been quickly removed thanks to the excellent heating and the many boxes she'd already shifted today—and yet another box lay ready for her attention. Her hair was piled up on top of her head, and the local radio station filled the room via her phone and a set of small speakers she'd purchased before she'd realised she had absolutely no money.

But she was glad for her previous financial frivolity. This massive house was creaky and echoey, and she'd hated how empty it had felt on her first day, when she'd been sorting through boxes wearing a pencil skirt, heels and a blouse with a bow—in total silence.

Bizarre how such an overflowing house could feel so empty, but it did.

Music helped. A little.

Now, on day three of her new job, already many

boxes lay flattened in the foyer. The shredder had disposed of old takeaway menus and shoe catalogues and local newspapers. And she'd labelled a handful of empty boxes for donations. Several were already full with books and random bits and pieces: a man's silk tie, a mass-produced ceramic vase, eleven tea towels from the Edinburgh Military Tattoo—and so much more. It was nearly impossible to categorise the items, although she'd tried.

But much of the boxes' content was, as Hugh had told her, junk. The packaging for electronic items, without the items themselves. Gossip magazines from ten years ago, with British reality TV stars she didn't recognise on the covers. Sugar and salt packets. Pens that didn't work. Dried-out mascara and nail polish bottles.

It was all so random.

Initially she'd approached each box with enthusiasm. What was she going to learn about the person who'd packed all these boxes from *this* box?

But each box gave little away.

There was no theme, there were no logical groupings or collections, and so far there was absolutely nothing personal. Not even one scribble on a takeaway menu.

Hugh hadn't given anything away, either.

It was hard in this house, with all its mysterious

boxes, not to think about the rather interesting and mysterious man who owned them all.

Were they *his* boxes?

April didn't think so. That morning in the kitchen, those clear but sparse directions and neat instructions had not indicated a man who collected such clutter. There was something terribly structured about the man: he exuded organisation and an almost regimented calm.

But that had changed when he'd shown her this room. The instant he'd opened the door he'd become tense. His body, his words. His gaze.

It had been obvious he'd wanted to leave, and he had as soon as humanly possible.

So, no, the boxes weren't his.

But they didn't belong to a stranger, either— because the boxes meant *something* to Hugh Bennell.

Her guess was that they belonged to a woman. The magazines, toiletries... But who?

His wife? Ex-wife? Mother? Sister? Friend?

So—with enthusiasm—April had decided to solve the mystery of the boxes.

But with box after box the mystery steadfastly remained and her enthusiasm rapidly waned.

On the radio, a newsreader read the ten o'clock news in a lovely, clipped British accent.

Only ten a.m.?

Her self-determined noon lunchbreak felt a lifetime away.

April sighed and straightened her shoulders, then carefully sliced open the brown packing tape of her next box.

On top lay empty wooden photo frames, one with a crack through the glass. And beneath that lay two phone books—the thick, heavy type that had used to be delivered before everyone had started searching for numbers online.

The unbroken wooden frames would go to the 'donate' box, and the phone books into the recycling. But as she walked out into the foyer, to add the books to the already mountainous recycling pile, a piece of card slipped out from between the pages.

April knelt to pick it up. It was an old and yellowed homemade bookmark, decorated with a child's red thumbprints in the shape of lopsided hearts.

Happy Mothering Sunday!
Love Hugh

The letters were in neat, thick black marker—the work of a school or kindergarten teacher.

And just like that she'd solved the mystery.

She started a new category: *Hugh.*

She wasn't making a decision on that bookmark, no matter what he said.

She'd let him know in her summarising email that evening.

* * *

The email pinged into Hugh's inbox shortly before five p.m. As it had the previous two days at approximately the same time, with the same subject line and the day's date. Exactly as he'd specified—which he appreciated.

She did insist on prefacing her emails with a bit of chatter, but she'd stuck to his guidelines for updating him on her progress.

Which was slower than he'd hoped. Although he didn't think that was April's fault—more his own desire for the house to be magically emptied as rapidly as possible.

That option still existed, of course. He'd researched a business that would come and collect all his mother's boxes and take them away. It would probably only take a day.

But he just couldn't bring himself to do that.

He hated those boxes—hated that stuff. Hated that his mother had been so consumed by it.

Despite it being junk, despite the way the boxes weighed so heavily upon him—both literally and figuratively—it just felt...

As if it would be disrespectful.

Hi Hugh,
I've found a bookmark today—photo attached—and I've put it aside for you. If I find anything similar I'll let you know.

Otherwise all going well. About two thirds through this room...

Hugh didn't read the rest. Instead he clicked open the attachment.

A minute later his boots thumped heavily against the steps up to his mother's front door. It was freezing in the evening darkness—he hadn't bothered to grab a coat for the very short journey—but the foyer was definitely a welcome relief as he let himself in.

April was still in the kitchen, her coat halfway on, obviously about to leave.

'Don't panic—I didn't throw it out,' she said.

'Throw what out?' he asked.

He hadn't seen her since that first morning, and she looked different in jeans and jumper—younger, actually. Her cheek was smudged with dust, her hair not entirely contained in the knot on top of her head.

'The bookmark,' she said. 'I'll just go grab it for you.'

'No,' he said. 'Don't.'

She'd already taken a handful of steps, and now stood only an arm's length before him.

'Okay,' she said. She inclined her chin in a direction over his shoulder. 'It's in a box out there. I've labelled it "Hugh". I'll just chuck anything in there that I think you should have a look at.'

'No,' he said again. 'Don't.'

Now she seemed to realise what he was saying.

Or at least she was no longer wilfully ignoring him. He knew how clear he'd been: with the exception of any paperwork that included personal details, April was to donate or trash *everything*.

'Are you sure?'

Hugh shrugged. 'It's just a badly painted bookmark.'

Up until a few minutes ago he'd had no recollection of that piece of well-intentioned crafting, so his life would definitely be no lesser with it gone.

'I wasn't just talking about the bookmark,' April said. 'I meant anything like that. I'm sure more sentimental bits and pieces are going to turn up. And what about photos? I found some photo frames today, so I expect eventually I'll find—'

'Photos can go in the bin,' he said.

Hugh shoved his hands in his jeans pockets. Again, he just wanted to be out of this place. But he didn't leave.

April was watching him carefully, concern in her clear blue gaze. He was shifting his weight from foot to foot. Fidgeting. He *never* fidgeted.

He wasn't himself in this house. With all this stuff. Now that the boxes had necessarily flowed into the foyer behind him the clutter was *everywhere*.

April had left an empty coffee mug on the kitchen sink.

Now he skirted around her, making his way to

the other side of the counter, grabbed the mug and opened the dishwasher. It was empty.

'I've just been hand-washing,' April said. 'I can wash that before I go—don't worry about it.'

Hugh ignored her, stuck the plug in the sink and turned on the hot water. Beneath the sink he found dishwashing liquid, and squirted it into the steaming water.

As the suds multiplied he was somewhat aware of April shrugging off her coat. He had no idea why it was so important for him to clean this mug, but it was.

'You can go,' he said, cleaning out the coffee marks from inside the mug. He realised it wasn't one of his mother's—it was printed with the logo of a Fremantle sporting team he didn't recognise and had a chip in the handle. It was April's.

He rinsed the mug in hot water and placed it on the dish rack.

Immediately it was picked up again—by April.

She was standing right beside him, tea towel in hand, busily drying the mug.

He hadn't noticed her move so close.

She didn't look at him, her concentration focused on her task. Her head was bent, and a long tendril of dark hair curled down to her nape.

This close, he could see the dust decorating her

hair, a darker smudge creating a streak across her cheekbone.

She turned, looking directly at him.

She was tall, he realised, even without her heels.

Today her lips weren't glossy, and he realised she probably wasn't wearing make-up. Her eyelashes were no longer the blackest black; her skin wasn't magazine-perfect.

She didn't look better—or worse. Just different. And it was that difference he liked.

That she'd surprised him.

He hadn't been able to imagine her unpacking boxes—but she looked just as comfortable today as she had in her sharp suit. And her gaze was just as strong, just as direct.

He realised he liked that, too.

It should have been an uncomfortable and un-wanted realisation. Maybe it was—or it would be later. When his brain wasn't cluttered with boxes and forgotten bookmarks and had room for logic and common sense...and remembering who he was. Who *she* was.

Boss. Employee...

For now, he simply looked at the surprising woman beside him.

'I know this is your mum's house,' she said. 'I get that this must be difficult for you.'

Her words were soft and gentle. They still cut deep.

But they shouldn't—and his instinct was to disagree. *They're just boxes. It's just stuff. It's not difficult in any way at all.*

He said nothing.

'Do you want me to come back tomorrow?'

Had she thought he might fire her over the bookmark?

He nodded sharply, without hesitation. Despite how uncomfortable her kind words had made him. Despite how unlike himself she made him. How aware he was of her presence in this room and in this house. How aware he was of how close she stood to him.

'Okay,' she said. 'I'll leave my mug, then.'

He didn't look at her as she stepped around him and put the coffee mug into an overhead cupboard.

By the time she'd shrugged back into her coat, and arranged her letterbox-red knitted scarf he'd pulled himself together.

'See you tomorrow,' she said, with a smile that was bright.

And then she was gone, leaving Hugh alone with a sink full of disappearing bubbles.

April's roommate was asleep when she got home from stacking shelves at the supermarket, so she went into the communal living room to call her mum.

For once the room was empty—usually the

Shoreditch shared house tended to have random people dotted all over the place.

Evidence of the crowd of backpackers who lived here—three from Australia and two from South Africa—was scattered everywhere, though. Empty beer bottles on the cheap glass coffee table, along with a bowl of now stale chips—crisps, they were called here—and a variety of dirty plastic plates and cups. One of the other Aussie girls had had a friend dossing on the couch, and his sheets and blankets still lay tangled and shoved into a corner, waiting for someone magically to wash them and put them away.

Which would happen—eventually. April had learnt that someone would get sick of the mess, and then do a mad tidy-up—loudly and passive-aggressively.

On a couple of occasions in the two weeks she'd been here it had been her—a lifetime of a weekly house-cleaning service meant she definitely preferred things clean, even though she'd had to look up how to clean a shower on the internet. She'd then realised that her relatively advanced age—she was the oldest of the group by six years—meant that everyone expected her to be the responsible, tidy one who'd clean up after everyone else.

And that wasn't going to happen.

She was too busy working her two jobs and trying

to stay on top of her April Molyneux social media world to add unpaid cleaner to the mix. So she'd co-ordinated the group, they'd all agreed on a roster... and sometimes it was followed.

So April ignored the mess, cleared a spot on the couch and scrolled to her mum's number on her phone.

'Darling!'

It was eight a.m. in Perth, but her mum was always up early. She'd finally retired only recently, with April's eldest sister Ivy taking over the reins at Molyneux Mining. But so far her mother's retirement had seemed to involve several new roles on company boards and a more hands-on role in the investments of the Molyneux Trust.

So basically not a whole lot of retirement was going on for Irene Molyneux. Which did not come as a surprise to anyone.

'Hi, Mum,' April said. 'How's things?'

'Nate is speaking so well!' Irene said. 'Yesterday he said "Can I have a biscuit, please?" Isn't that amazing?'

Irene was also embracing the chance to spend more time with her two-year-old grandson. After five minutes of Nate stories, her mum asked April how she was doing.

'Good,' she said automatically. And then, 'Okay, I guess...'

'What's wrong?'

And so April told her about the bookmark, and her new boss's crystal-clear directive. She didn't mention the details, though—like the sadness she'd seen in Hugh's eyes in the kitchen. His obvious pain.

Her mother was typically no-nonsense. 'If he isn't sentimental, it isn't your role to be.'

But that was the thing—she wasn't convinced he didn't care. Not even close.

'I don't know. It just doesn't feel right.'

'Mmm...' her mother said. 'You can always quit.'

But... 'It pays almost double what I was earning at my last placement.'

'I know,' Irene said.

Her mum didn't say anything further—but April knew what she was thinking. She was torn between supporting April in her goal to pay off her credit card and live independently—a goal she'd supported once she'd been reassured April wasn't going to end up homeless—and solving all her problems. With money.

Which was understandable, really. Her mother had, after all, financially supported April her entire life. And April honestly had never questioned it. She was rich—it was just who she was. Her bottomless credit cards had just come with the territory.

But, really, the only thing she'd ever done that really deserved any payment was her work for the

Molyneux Foundation. And besides a few meetings she'd probably spent maybe an hour or two a day working for the foundation—with a big chunk of that time focused on making sure she looked as picture-perfect as possible in photos.

It had been a cringe-worthy, shamefully spoiled existence.

'You understand why I need to do this, right? All of this: living here, living on *my* money, living without the Molyneux name?'

'Yes,' Irene said. 'And you know I admire what you're doing. And I'm a little ashamed of myself for being so worried about you.'

This was cringe-worthy too—how little her family expected of her. Her fault as well, of course.

'But that's my job,' Irene continued. 'I'm your mum. I'm supposed to worry. And I'm supposed to want to fix things. But, if I put that aside, here's my non-mum advice—keep the job. Keep working hard, pay off your debt and move out of that awful shared house. It'll make me feel better once you're living in your own place.'

'Yes, Mum,' April said, smiling. 'I'll do my best.'

And then she remembered something she'd been thinking about earlier.

'Hey, Mum, did *you* keep that type of stuff? Stuff that we all made at school—you know, gifts for Mother's Day? Finger paintings? That sort of stuff?'

Irene laughed. 'No! I'm probably a terrible person, but I remember smuggling all that stuff out to the bin under cover of darkness.'

They talked for a while longer, but later, when April had ended the call and gone to bed, her thoughts wandered back to that faded little bookmark Hugh had once given to his mother.

Was she just being sentimental? She wasn't sure how she felt about her mum not keeping any of her childhood art—but then, had it bothered her until now? She hadn't even noticed. Maybe Hugh was right—maybe it *was* just a badly painted bookmark.

But that was the thing—the way Hugh had reacted...the way he'd raced to see her immediately, and the way he'd washed her Dockers mug as if the weight of the world had been on his shoulders...

It felt like so much more.

CHAPTER FOUR

'Hugh?'

'We must've lost him.'

'Should we reschedule? We can't make a decision without him.'

Belatedly Hugh registered what the conference call voices were saying.

He'd tuned out at some point. In fact, he could barely remember what the meeting was about. He glanced at his laptop screen.

Ah. App bug fixes. And something about the latest iOS upgrade.

Not critically important to his business, but important enough that he should be paying attention.

He *always* paid attention.

The meeting ended with his presumed disappearance, and his flat was silent.

He pushed back his chair and headed for the kitchen, leaning against the counter as his kettle boiled busily.

He'd left his tea mug in the sink, as he always did.

He reused it throughout the day, and chucked it in the dishwasher each night.

Why had he cared about April's mug?

He was neat. He knew that. Extremely neat. The perfect contrast to his mother and her overwhelming messiness.

Although, to be fair, his mother hadn't always been like that.

At first it had just been clutter. It had only been later that the dishes had begun to pile in the sink and mounds of clothes had remained unwashed. And by then he'd been old enough to help. So he'd taken over—diligently cleaning around all his mum's things: her 'treasures' and her 'we might need it one days', her flotsam and jetsam and her 'there's a useful article/recipe/tip in that' magazines, newspapers and books.

But he wasn't obsessive—at least not to the level of compulsively cleaning an employee's coffee mug.

It had been odd. For him and for April.

He didn't feel good about that.

He didn't know this woman at all.

That had been deliberate. He hadn't wanted to use the Precise HR Department, or reach out to his team for recommendations of casual workers, university students or backpackers—he hadn't wanted anyone he knew or worked with to know about what was he was doing.

But the fact was someone needed to know what he was doing in order to actually do it—and that person was April Spencer.

And so she knew about his mother's hoard and would know it better than anyone ever had. Even him.

That sat uncomfortably. Hugh had spent much of his life hiding his mother's hoard. It didn't feel right to invite somebody in. Literally to lay it all out to be seen—to be judged.

His mum had loved him, had worked so hard, and had provided him with all she could and more on a minimal wage and without any support from his father. She didn't deserve to be judged as anything less than she had been: a great mum. A great woman.

Her hoard had not defined her, but if people had known of it…

The kettle had boiled and Hugh made his tea, leaving the teabag hanging over the edge of his cup.

April had offered to leave yesterday.

But he'd rejected her offer without consideration, and now, even with time, he knew it had been the right decision.

If it wasn't April it would be someone else. At least April wasn't connected to his work or anyone he knew. Anyone who'd known his mother.

She was a temporary worker—travelling, probably. She'd soon be back in Australia, or off to her next working holiday somewhere sunnier than London, and she'd take her knowledge of his mother's secret hoard with her.

His phone buzzed—a text message.

Drinks after work at The Saint?

It was a group message to the cyclists he often rode with a few mornings a week. He liked them. They were dedicated, quick, and they pushed him to get stronger, and faster.

He replied.

Sorry, can't make it.

He always declined the group's social invitations. He liked riding with them, but he didn't do pubs and clubs. Or any place there was likely to be an unpredictable crowd—he never had, and in fact he'd never been able to—not even as a child. He avoided any crowd, but enclosed crowds—exactly as one might find in a pub—made him feel about as comfortable as a room full of his mother's boxes.

He actually wasn't sure which had come first: Had he inherited his crowd-related anxiety from his compulsive hoarder mother, or had his hatred of bustling crowds stemmed from the nightmares he'd once had of being suffocated beneath an avalanche of boxes?

It didn't really matter—the outcome was the same: Hugh Bennell wasn't exactly a party animal.

Fortunately Hugh's repeated refusals to socialise didn't seem to bother his cycling group. He was aware, however, that they all thought he was a bit weird.

But that wasn't an unfamiliar sensation for him— he'd been the weird kid at school too. After all, it hadn't been as if he could ever invite anybody over to his place to play.

Want to come over and see my mum's hoard?

Yeah. That had never happened. He'd never allowed it to happen.

His doorbell rang.

Hugh glanced at his watch. It was early afternoon—not even close to the time when packages were usually delivered. And he certainly wasn't expecting anybody.

Tea still in hand, he headed for the door. It could only be a charity collector, or somebody distributing religious pamphlets.

Instead it was April.

She stood in her coat and scarf, carrying a box.

A box labelled '*Hugh*'.

Hugh's eyes narrowed when he saw her.

April knew she wasn't supposed to be down here, but she just hadn't been able to simply send an email.

He wore a T-shirt, black jeans and an unzipped hoodie, and he held a cup of tea in one hand. He was barefoot and his hair, as she'd come to expect, was scruffy—as if he'd woken up and simply run a hand through it. Yesterday he'd been smooth-shaven, but today the stubble was back—and, as she'd also come to expect, she really rather liked it.

Hugh Bennell seemed to be in a permanent state of sexy dishevelment, and she'd put money on it— if she had any—that he had no idea.

But now was not the time to be pondering any of this.

'Ms Spencer?' he prompted.

Ms Spencer—not April. He definitely wasn't impressed.

She swallowed. 'I'm resigning,' she said. 'I didn't just want to put it in an email.'

A gust of wind whipped down from the street and through the doorway. Despite her coat, April shivered.

Hugh noticed.

He stepped back and gestured for her to come inside.

April blinked—she hadn't expected him to do that. She had a suspicion *he* hadn't either, although his gaze remained unreadable.

Somehow as she stepped past Hugh, slightly awkwardly with the large box, she managed to brush against him—just her upper arm, briefly against his chest. It was the most minimal of touches—made minuscule once combined with her heavy wool coat and Hugh's combination of T-shirt and hoodie. And yet she blushed.

April felt her cheeks go hot and her skin—despite all the layers—prickled with awareness.

How ridiculous. Really only their clothing had touched. Nothing more.

She forced her attention to her surroundings, not looking anywhere near Hugh.

His basement flat was compact and immaculate. Two bikes hung neatly on a far wall, but otherwise the walls were completely empty. In fact the whole place felt empty—there wasn't a trinket or a throw cushion in sight. The only evidence of occupation was the desk, pushed right up against the front window, and its few scattered papers, sticky note pads and pens were oddly reassuring in their imperfection.

They were standing near his taupe-coloured couches, but Hugh didn't sit so neither did she.

Her blush had faded, so she could finally look at him again. Even if it was more in the direction of his shoulder rather than at his eyes. His *knowing* eyes?

She refused to consider it.

'Anyway,' April said, deliberately brisk, 'I found

some more things today. A couple of photos of you and your mum and a birthday card.'

She shook her head sharply when Hugh went to speak. She didn't want to hear his spiel again.

'And, look…maybe I should've chucked them out, as you've insisted. But then I found one of those old plastic photo negative barrels—you know? And it had a lock of baby's hair in it.'

She met his gaze.

'*A lock of hair*, Hugh. Yours, I think. And then I was done. I'm not throwing *that* out. That's not my responsibility, and it's definitely not my decision.'

She carefully put the box on Hugh's coffee table.

'So there's the box with your things in it. You can throw it straight in the skip if you want, but *I* couldn't.' She turned around as she straightened, meeting Hugh's gaze again. He gave nothing away. 'I've finished that first reception room, and I've organised for the charity donations to be collected tomorrow.'

Still in her coat and scarf, she felt uncomfortably warm—and not entirely because of the central heating.

'I'd better get going.'

'No notice?' Hugh asked.

His tone was calm and measured. *He* definitely wasn't blushing, or paying any attention when April did.

She was being ridiculous.

'No,' April said. 'I didn't see the point. Clearly I'm unsuitable for the position.'

'What if I made the position suitable?' he said, not missing a beat.

'Pardon me?'

'What if I said you didn't have to make all the decisions any more?' He spoke with perfect calm.

'So I can have a "Hugh" box?'

He nodded. 'Yes.'

'And you'll come sort through it each day?'

Now he shook his head. 'No. I'll come and throw it in the skip each day. But at least *you* wouldn't have to.'

No. That still didn't feel right. April wasn't sure she could let that happen...

Wait. It wasn't her call. It *so* wasn't her call.

And that was all she'd asked for—not to be the decision-maker.

The job paid well. And it wasn't very difficult— now Hugh had removed the requirement to throw out intensely personal items.

And she still had her credit card debt, still had a manky shared house to move out of.

It was a no-brainer.

And yet she hesitated.

The reason stood in front of her. Making her belly heat and her skin warm simply with his presence.

His *oblivious* presence, it would seem.

In which case…what was she worried about?

She knew she didn't want to walk straight from Evan and into another relationship, and that certainly didn't seem to be on offer here.

Hugh was looking at her with his compelling eyes, waiting not entirely patiently for a response. He did *not* look like a man who enjoyed waiting.

April smiled.

It had been fifteen years since she'd been single. It was probably normal that her hormones were being slightly over the top in the vicinity of a demonstrably handsome man.

It was nothing more.

'Deal,' she said.

She had nothing to worry about.

But then Hugh smiled back—and it was the first time she'd seen him smile both with his divine mouth and with his remarkable eyes.

Probably nothing.

On the following day there was nothing to put into the 'Hugh' box.

So April emailed Hugh with her daily update, put on her coat, went home to her still messy shared house and ate soup that had come out of a can while her housemates drank wine that came out of a box. Later, when her housemates headed out to a bar,

April walked around the corner to her local super-market and stacked more cans of soup—and lots of other things—until the early hours of the morning.

The next day, at the Islington end-of-terrace house, April brewed a strong coffee in her Dockers mug, running her thumb across the chip on the handle as she always did. She then placed it on the marble benchtop just where the light hit it, artistically—or as artistically as a coffee mug could be placed—and took a photo.

Really need this today! #workinghard #ilovecaffeine #tooearly

Then she scheduled the post for shortly after Perth would be waking up.

She knew she'd get lots of questions about what she was working so hard on—which was the point. And she'd be vague, and everyone would assume it was something super-exotic—like a fundraising gala event or a photo shoot.

Not unpacking boxes in a grand old dusty house in London.

April smiled.

Part of her wanted to tell her followers *exactly* what she was doing. To tell them that she actually *hadn't* been doing totally fine after Evan had left her, that she'd run away from everyone who loved her and for the first time in her life had realised how privileged she actually was.

But the rest of her knew she had commitments. Knew that the Molyneux Foundation's sponsors hadn't signed up for her to have an early midlife crisis.

And mostly she knew that she wasn't ready to make any big decisions just yet.

She still hadn't really got her head around the fact that she was single.

Of course she'd looked at other men since she'd starting going out with Evan. She'd even had men flirt with her—quite often, really. Possibly because of her sparkling personality—more likely because of all the dollar signs she represented.

But, regardless whether she'd thought some guy was hot, or if some guy had thought *she* was hot—or just rich—it hadn't mattered. She'd been with Evan. So she'd been able to acknowledge a handsome man objectively and then efficiently deflect any flirting that veered beyond harmless.

Because she'd always had Evan.

She'd always loved Evan.

And now that she *didn't* have Evan, meeting another man wasn't on April's radar. It hadn't even been on her radar as something *not* to do—she hadn't even thought about it. It had been too impossible.

Until she'd met Hugh. And then it hadn't. It hadn't felt impossible at all.

But it still *was*, of course.

Totally impossible. As she'd reminded herself in Hugh's flat, she wasn't going to walk from a fifteen-year relationship into another. And—and this scenario felt far more likely—she *definitely* wasn't going to walk from one rejection straight into another one.

There were lots of things she had learnt she could cope with: having no money, working two jobs—two *labour intensive* jobs, no less—living in a shared house at age thirty-two and having her family on the other side of the world.

But she knew utterly and completely that she couldn't cope with another man rejecting her.

I don't love you.

How could those words still hurt so much?

She didn't miss Evan. She understood that their relationship had reached its inevitable conclusion. She definitely didn't want to be with him any more.

But… *I don't love you.*

And he never had.

That pain didn't just go away.

Hugh was already boiling the kettle in his mother's kitchen when April arrived the next morning.

Her gaze flicked over him as she walked into the

room, her bag slung over her long coat, her scarf in shades of green today.

'Good morning,' she said, in that polished, friendly tone he was becoming familiar with. She was good at sounding comfortable even when she wasn't.

He could see the questions in her gaze and the instant tension in her stride as she walked towards the bar stools tucked beneath the marble counter.

'Morning,' Hugh said as she dumped her bag on a chair and then shrugged out of her coat. 'I thought I'd help move those heavy boxes.'

Her email last night had explained that she'd found some boxes that would need two people to lift them. He'd considered contacting the temp agency to recruit someone, and then had realised that to do so would be preposterous. He was thirty-six, fit and he lived ten metres away. *He* could move the damn boxes. They were, no matter how much he seemed needlessly to over-complicate them, just boxes. He didn't have to deal with any of the stuff inside them.

She nodded. 'Great!' she said, although he couldn't tell if she meant it. 'I thought you'd just organise someone to come and help me.'

'I did,' he said, then pointed towards his chest. 'Me.'

Her smile now was genuine. And lovely. He'd thought that every time he'd seen her smile. It was another reason he'd considered calling the temp office. But similarly—just as the boxes were only boxes—a smile was only a smile. It, and his admiration of it, meant nothing more.

'It shouldn't take long. I could probably do it myself, but I'd hate to drop one of the boxes and break something.'

The kettle clicked as it finished boiling.

'Doesn't matter if you do,' Hugh said. 'But still—ask me to help move anything heavy, regardless. I don't want you to hurt yourself.'

April blinked as if he'd said something unexpected. 'Okay,' she said.

They took their coffee into the second reception room.

As always, the cluttered space made Hugh feel stiff and antsy—as if he could run a marathon on the adrenalin that shot through his veins.

So far April had cleared only a small section of this room. Once it had been his mum and Len's TV room. They'd sat on the large, plush couch, their legs propped on matching ottomans, dinner balanced on their laps.

The couch was still there—one arm visible amongst the bevy of boxes.

The heavy boxes were near the window. They were much bigger than the boxes that had filled the first room—probably five or more times their size—and stacked only two high.

It was the top boxes that April wanted to be lifted down.

Coffee placed carefully on the floor, it was easy for the pair of them to lift the boxes: one, two...

For the third, they both had to reach awkwardly around it, tucked away as it was between the heavy curtains and another wall of boxes.

In doing so their fingers brushed against each other, along the far side of the box.

Only for a second—or not even that long.

Barely long enough to be noticed—but Hugh did.

Her hand felt cool and soft. Her nails glossy and smooth beneath his palm.

His gaze darted to April's, but she was too busy lifting the box to pay any attention at all.

Or too busy deliberately looking busy.

He suspected the latter. He'd noticed her reaction in his flat when she'd so briefly brushed against him. Her cheeks had blushed pink in an instant.

He'd reacted, too.

It was strange, really, for his blood to heat like that from such an innocent touch.

He hadn't expected it.

Not that he hadn't continued to notice April's attractiveness. It would be impossible not to. She was beautiful in a classic, non-negotiable way—but beauty was not something Hugh should be paying much attention to when it came to a woman working for him.

So he'd made sure he hadn't.

Except for when she'd stood beside him at the sink a few nights ago, when his thoughts had been jumbled and unfocused. Then the shape of her neck, of her jaw, the profile of her nose and chin...

Yes, he'd noticed.

But, more, he'd noticed her empathy. And her sympathy. Even if he had welcomed neither.

Nor welcomed his attraction to her.

He didn't want complications. Right now—getting this house cleaned out—or ever.

His lifestyle was planned and structured to avoid complications.

Even when he dated women it was only ever for the briefest of times—brevity, he'd discovered, avoided the complications that were impossible for him: commitment, cohabiting, planning a future together...

Relationships were all about complications, and to Hugh complications were clutter.

And he was determined to live a clutter-free life.

But today contact with April's skin had again made his blood heat and his belly tighten.

He should go.

They'd moved the box to where April had directed, so Hugh headed for the door.

'Don't forget your coffee,' April said.

He turned and saw she held the two mugs in her hands—the one for him printed with agapanthus.

He should go—he could make his own coffee downstairs. There was nothing to be gained by staying, and as always he had so much on his to-do list today.

But he realised, surprised, that the boxes that surrounded him weren't compelling him to leave. At some point the tension that had been driving him from this house had abated.

It was still there, but no longer overpowering. Nor, it seemed, was it insurmountable.

So he found himself accepting his mug from April. A woman who, with no more than her smile and against all his better judgement, had somehow compelled him to stay.

He hadn't been supposed to stay.

April had honestly expected Hugh to take his coffee and head on down to his basement apartment.

But instead he'd taken his mug and approached the first box she'd planned to go through—its top already sliced open, the flaps flipped back against the thick cardboard sides.

For a moment it had looked as if he was going to

start looking through the box. He'd stepped right up beside it, his spare hand extended, and then he had simply let it fall back against his jean-clad thigh.

Now he brought his mug to his lips, his gaze, as usual, impossible to interpret.

'You really don't like these boxes,' April said. Her words were possibly unwise—but they'd just slipped out.

Hugh Bennell intrigued her. And not just his looks—or his touch, however accidental. But who he was and what all these boxes meant to him.

The boxes, of course, intrigued her too.

He shot a look in her direction, raising an eyebrow. 'No.'

And that was that. No elaboration.

So April simply got to work.

Hugh walked a few steps away, propping his backside against the only available arm of the sofa. Boxes were stacked neatly on the seat cushions beside him.

This box was full of clothes. A woman's. April hadn't come across women's clothes before, and the discovery of the brightly coloured silks and satins made her smile and piqued her interest.

She held a top against herself: a cream sheer blouse with thick black velvet ribbon tied into a bow at the neck. It was too small for April—smaller even than the sample size clothing she'd used to have sent to her by designers before she'd given up on starving herself.

'Was this your mum's?' April asked, twisting to face Hugh.

She absolutely knew it wasn't her place to ask him, but she just couldn't *not*.

It was too weird to be standing in this room with Hugh, in silence, surrounded by all this stuff that meant something to him but absolutely nothing to her. And *she* was the one sorting through it.

Hugh didn't even blink. 'All clothing is to be donated,' he said.

'That wasn't why I was asking,' April said.

She tossed the shirt into the 'donate' box in the centre of the room. Soon after followed a deep pink shift dress, a lovely linen shawl and a variety of printed T-shirts. Next April discovered a man's leather bomber jacket that was absolutely amazing but about a hundred sizes too big.

Regardless, April tried it on. Felt compelled to.

Was it disrespectful to try it on?

Possibly. Probably.

But Hugh was about to donate it all, anyway. *He* was the one who insisted it was all junk, all worthless.

Maybe this was how she could trigger a reaction from this tall, silent man?

It was unequivocally a bad idea, but she spent her

days unpacking boxes and her evenings stacking shelves. Mostly in silence.

Maybe she was going stir crazy, but she needed to see what Hugh would do.

She just didn't buy it that he didn't care about this stuff. So far his measured indifference had felt decidedly unconvincing.

She *had* to call his bluff.

'I'm not paying you to play dress-up,' Hugh pointed out from behind her.

His tone was neutral.

She spun around to show him the oversized jacket. 'Spoilsport,' she said with a deliberate grin, catching his gaze.

If he was just going to stand there she couldn't cope with all this silence and gloom. Her sisters had always told her she was the *sunny* sister. That she could walk into a room and brighten it with her smile.

It had always sounded rather lame—and to be honest part of her *had* wondered what that said about her in comparison to *clever* Ivy or *artistic* Mila. Was it really such an achievement to be good at smiling?

It had been a moot point in the months since Evan had left, anyway.

Until now. Now, this darkly moody man felt like a challenge for sunny April.

Acutely aware that this might all backfire horribly, but incapable of stopping herself in the awkward silence, she playfully tossed her hair in the way of a supermodel.

'What do you think?'

What would he do? Smile? Shout? Leave?

Fire her?

Hugh's shake of the head was barely perceptible.

But…was that a quirk to his lips?

Yes. It was definitely there.

April's smile broadened.

'Fair enough,' she said, shrugging her shoulders and then tossing the jacket into the 'donate' box. 'How about this?' she asked, randomly grabbing the next item of clothing in the box.

A boat-neck blouse, in a shiny fabric with blue and white stripes. But too small. Which April realised…too late.

Hands stuck up in the air, fabric bunched around her shoulders on top of her T-shirt, April went completely still.

'Dammit!' she muttered.

She hadn't been entirely sure of her plan, but becoming trapped in cheap satin fabric was definitely not part of it.

She wiggled again, trying to dislodge the blouse, but it didn't shift.

Her T-shirt had ridden up at least a little. April

could feel cool air against a strip of skin above the waistband of her jeans.

Mortified, she struggled again, twisting away from where she knew Hugh stood, feeling unbelievably silly and exposed.

'Stay still,' he said, suddenly impossibly close. Behind her.

April froze. She was blindfolded by the stupid top but she could sense his proximity. His height. His width.

His fingers hooked under the striped fabric, right at her shoulders. He was incredibly careful, gently moving the fabric upwards. Her arms were still trapped. It was almost unbearable: the touch of his fingers, his closeness, her vulnerability.

She wanted him to just yank it off over her head. To get this over with.

No, she didn't.

The fabric had cleared her shoulders now, and he moved closer still to help tug it over her arms, where the top was still wrapped tightly.

Now his fingers brushed against the bare skin of her arms. Only as much as necessary—and that didn't feel like anywhere near enough.

He was so close behind her that if she shifted backwards even the slightest amount she would be pressed right up against him. Back to chest.

It seemed a delicious possibility.

It seemed, momentarily, as she was wrapped in the temporary dark, a viable option.

And then the blouse was pulled free.

April gasped as the room came back into focus. Directly in front of her were heavy navy curtains, closed, obscured by an obstacle course of cardboard boxes.

She spun around.

'Thank you—' she began.

Then stopped.

Hugh was still so close. Closer than he'd ever been before. Tall enough and near enough that he needed to look down at her and she needed to tilt her chin up.

She explored his face. The sharpness of his nose, the thick slash of his eyebrows, the strength of his jaw. This close she could see delicate lines bracketing his lips, a freckle on his cheek, a rogue grey hair amongst the stubble.

He was studying her, too. His gaze took in her eyes, her cheeks, her nose. Her lips.

There it was.

Not subtle now, or easily dismissed as imagination as it had been down in his basement apartment. Or every other time they'd been in the same room together.

But it *had* been there, she realised. Since the first time they'd met.

That focus. That…intent.

That *heat*.

Between them. Within her.

It made her pulse race and caused her to become lost in his gaze when he finally wrenched his away from her lips.

Since they'd met his eyes had revealed little. Enough for her to know, deep in her heart, that he wasn't as hard and unfeeling as he so steadfastly attempted to be. It was why she'd known she couldn't be responsible for the disposal of his mother's memories.

And maybe that was what had obscured what she saw so clearly now. Or at least had allowed her to question it.

Electricity practically crackled between them. It seemed ludicrous that she hadn't known before. That she'd ever doubted it.

Hugh Bennell *wanted* her.

And she wanted him. In a way that left her far more exposed than her displaced T-shirt.

But then he stepped back. His gaze was shuttered again.

'You okay?' he asked, his voice deep and gravelly.

No.

'Yes,' she said, belatedly realising he was referring to the stripy top and not to what had just happened between them.

Way too late she tugged down her T-shirt, and blushed when his gaze briefly followed the movement of her hands. Then it shifted away.

Not swiftly, as if he'd been caught out or was embarrassed. Just away.

He didn't look at her again as he went over to the box April had been emptying.

Without hesitation he reached in, grabbing a large handful of clothing and directly deposited it into the 'donate' box. Then, with brisk efficiency, he went through the remainder of the box: ancient yellow newspapers to the recycling pile, a toaster with a severed electrical cord to the bin, encyclopaedias with blue covers and gold-edged pages on top of the clothing in the donation box.

April had been boxing books separately, but she didn't say a word.

The donation box was now full, already packed with yesterday's miscellanea, and Hugh lifted it effortlessly.

April followed him into the foyer and directed him to where she'd like the box left, ready for the next visit by the red-and-white charity collection truck.

'Thank you,' she said.

He shrugged. 'I just want this stuff gone.'

She nodded. 'I'd better get back to work, then.'

Finally her temporary inertia had lifted, and reality—the most obvious being that it was her job to empty these boxes, not Hugh's—had reasserted itself.

Although amidst that reality the crackling tension between them still remained.

April didn't know what to do with it.

Hugh seemed unaffected, but April knew for certain that he wasn't unaware.

'These clothes aren't my mum's,' he said suddenly. 'I have no idea who they belong to. I have no idea what most of this stuff is, or why the hell my mum needed to keep it all so badly.'

April nodded again. His tone had hardened as he spoke, frustration fracturing his controlled facade.

'She was more than all this stuff. Much more.' He shook his head. 'Why couldn't she see that?'

Hugh met her gaze again, but April knew he'd asked the most rhetorical of questions.

'I'll get this stuff out of your house,' she said. She promised.

'*Her* house,' he clarified.

And then, without another word, he was gone.

CHAPTER FIVE

HUGH HADN'T SLEPT WELL.

He'd woken late, so he'd been too late to join the group he normally rode with on a Wednesday, so instead he'd headed out alone. Today that was his preference anyway.

Because it was later, traffic was heavier.

It was also extremely cold, and the roads were slick with overnight rain.

London could be dangerous for a cyclist, and Hugh understood and respected this.

It was partly why he often chose to ride in groups, despite his general preference for solitude. Harried drivers were forced to give pairs or long lines of bikes room on the road, and were less likely to scrape past mere millimetres from Hugh's handlebars.

But other times—like this morning—his need to be alone trumped the safety of numbers.

Today he didn't want the buzz of conversation to surround him. Or for other cyclists to share some random anecdote or to espouse the awesomeness of their new carbon fibre wheels.

When he rode alone it was the beat of his own pulse that filled his ears, alongside the cadence of his breathing and the whir of the wheels.

Around him the cacophony of noise that was early-morning London simply receded.

It was just him and his bike and the road.

Hugh rode hard—hard enough to keep his mind blank and his focus only on the next stroke of the pedals.

Soon he was out of inner London, riding down the A24 against the flow of commuter traffic. He was warm with exertion, but the wind was still icy against his cheeks. The rest of his body was cloaked in jet-black full-length cycling pants, a long-sleeved jersey, gilet and gloves.

Usually by now the group would have begun to loop back, but today Hugh just kept on riding and riding, heading from busy roads to country lanes, losing track of time. Eventually he reached the Surrey Hills and their punishing inclines, relishing the burning of his lungs and the satisfying ache of his thighs and calves.

But midway up Box Hill, with his brain full of no more than his own thundering heartbeat, he stopped. On a whim, abruptly he violently twisted his cleats out of his pedals and yanked hard on the brakes until his bike was still. Then, standing beside his bike, he surveyed the rolling green patchwork of the Dorking valley as it stretched towards the South Downs beneath a clear blue sky. Out here, amongst woodland and sheep-dotted fields, London was thirty miles and a world away.

What was he doing?

He didn't have to check his watch to know he'd missed his morning teleconference. He'd miss his early-afternoon meetings too, given it would take him another two and a half hours to get home again.

Reception would be patchy up here, he knew, but still, he should at least try to email his assistant—who worked remotely from Lewisham—and ask her to clear his calendar for the rest of the day.

But he didn't.

He hadn't planned to ride this far, but he'd needed to. He'd needed to do something to ease the discontent that had kept him awake half the night—much of it spent pacing his lounge room floor.

Hugh didn't like how he felt. All agitated and uncertain.

He usually lived his life with such definition: he knew what he was doing, why he was doing it, and he always knew it was the right thing to do. Hugh made it his business to plan and prepare and analyse *everything*. It was why his business was so successful. He didn't make mistakes…he didn't get distracted.

His mother's house had always been the exception.

When she'd died he'd considered selling it. He'd been living in his own place in Primrose Hill, not far away.

But back then—as now—he just hadn't been able to.

For a man who prided himself on being the antithesis of his mother—on being a man who saw no value in objects and who ruthlessly protected his life from clutter—his attachment to the house was an embarrassing contradiction.

But he knew how much that house had meant to his mum. He knew exactly what it had represented.

For his mother it had been a place of love, after so many years of searching.

And for Hugh it had been where his mother had finally lived a life free of clutter—a life he had been sure she'd lost for ever. For more than a decade she'd been happy there, her hoard no more than a distant memory.

And so he'd kept it.

He'd ended up hoarding his mother's hoard. There was no other way to explain his three-year refusal to dispose of all that junk.

Even now, as April Spencer attempted to clean out his mother's house, he couldn't let it go.

A stranger—April—had seen that.

Why else would she be going to such lengths to save sentimental crap unless she'd sensed that he wasn't really ready to relinquish it?

And she was right. The original 'Hugh' box still remained as April had left it, cluttering up his coffee table in all its ironic glory.

He just hadn't been able to walk to the skip behind the house and throw it all away. It had felt impossible.

How pathetic.

Yesterday he'd helped April move those boxes in an effort to normalise the situation: to prove to himself that his visceral reaction to them could be overcome. Except he hadn't considered April. He hadn't considered his visceral reaction to *her*.

He hadn't considered that, while he might be able to dismiss his attraction to her as nothing when he spent only short periods of time with her, more time together might not be so manageable.

Because more time with her meant he'd seen another side of her: a mischievous forthrightness that really shouldn't have surprised him, given her refusal to follow his original instructions.

And he liked it. *A lot.*

He'd also liked it—a lot—when she'd got tangled up in that shirt.

He'd liked being so very close to her—close enough

to smell her shampoo and admire the Australian tan revealed below her bunched up T-shirt. Close enough to feel her shiver beneath his touch. To hear the acceleration of her breathing.

In those long moments after he'd helped her out of the blouse it had been as intimate as if he'd actually undressed her.

It had felt raw and naked—and incredibly intense. As if, had he touched her, they would've both lost control completely. And for those long moments he'd wanted nothing more than to lose control with April Spencer.

But Hugh Bennell *never* lost control.

And so he hadn't. He'd taken a step back, even though it had been harder than he would've liked.

He'd assessed the situation: April worked for him.

His priority was cleaning out his mother's house, not fraternising with his employees.

Besides, he suspected his reaction to April was somehow tangled up with his reaction to the boxes. Because it wasn't normal for him to have such a magnetic pull towards a woman. He was generally far more measured when he met a woman he liked. In fact he always 'met' the women he dated online.

It allowed for a certain level of…well, of *control*, really. He could set his expectations, as could the woman he was speaking too. There was never any confusion or miscommunication, or the risk of having anything misconstrued.

It was incredibly efficient.

But starting with physical attraction...*no*.

Although it had been difficult to remind himself why as he'd paced his parquet floor at three a.m.

His mind had been as full with thoughts of April as with his continued frustration over the house and all its boxes.

Mostly with April, actually.

The softness of her skin. The way her lips had parted infinitesimally as they'd gazed into each other's eyes. And that urge to lean forward and take what he knew she'd been offering had been so compelling it had felt inevitable...

No.

And so his bike ride. A bike ride to clear his mind of the clutter his mother's hoard and April were creating.

It had been a good plan, Hugh thought as he got back on his bike.

A total fail, though, in practice, with his brain still unable to let go of memories of warm skin and knowing blue eyes as he rode back down the hill, alongside the song of a skylark caught up in the breeze.

Mila: OMG Gorgeous!

April: That's one to save for his twenty-first! :)

April typed her instant messaging response to Ivy's gorgeous photo of her son, Nate, covered in bubbles in the bathtub. It felt like for ever since she'd spoken to both her sisters together.

April: How are sales going, Mila?

Mila had recently started mass-producing some of her ceramic work to keep up with sales at her small boutique pottery business.

Mila: Pretty good. I've experimented with pricing a bit. I'm still not sure how much people value handmade. So far it seems that the hand-glazing is the key, because...

Mila went into quite a lot of detail—as Mila always did when it came to her business—and then posted some photos she'd taken in her workshop.

April had always been proud of Mila—of both her sisters. She'd always admired how Mila had been so adamant that she'd build her business without the financial support of their mother, but until now April had never really had an issue with spending her family's money herself.

In fact it had taken her until her mid-twenties before she'd realised she should be doing a lot more with her good fortune than attending parties and buying everything she liked on every fashion festival catwalk.

And so she'd started the Molyneux Foundation.

She'd deliberately chosen not to be the face of the foundation because it wasn't about her. In fact she'd asked her mother to be the patron. But there was no question that it was April driving the foundation. It had become *her* project and, along with a small team, she'd made sure the foundation had continued to grow—and for every dollar donated to the foundation Molyneux Mining matched it twice over.

April had experimented with a few different ideas for the foundation—a website, later a blog—and by the time Instagram had gained popularity April had known exactly how to monetise it best to help the foundation. She'd had her team reaching out to any company that sold a product she could include in a photo, and she'd carefully curated the images to ensure that she mixed promotional pictures seamlessly in with those that were just her own.

And it had worked. She didn't think her mum had expected it to take off the way it had when April had talked her into the two-to-one deal, but it was certainly too late now!

She was incredibly proud of all the foundation had achieved, and of her role in that. But she'd still really just considered it a little side project. She was as hands-on as needed, but it was hardly a full-time job. She'd still had plenty of time to shop and socialise—and until Evan had left her it had never occurred to her to live without the Molyneux money.

The Molyneux money to which *she* had contributed in absolutely no way at all.

And the brittleness of all that—the fact that without the Molyneux money she had literally nothing... no means to support herself...not one thing she'd bought with money she'd actually earned herself— was quite frightening.

Ivy: How's the new job going?

April: Good. Mostly. Lots of boxes.

She'd love to post a photo to show the magnitude of the hoard to her sisters, but photography was one of the many things expressly forbidden by the confidentiality agreement she'd signed. Along with any discussion of the contents of the boxes.

April: My boss is interesting.

She'd typed that before she'd really thought about what she was doing.

Ivy: Oooh! Interesting-interesting? Or INTERESTING-interesting? ;-) ;-) ;-)

April: Both.

She'd never been good at keeping secrets from her sisters.

Mila: Photo?

April: No. I can't even tell you his name. But he's tall. Dark hair, dark eyes. Stubble. What do you call it...? Swarthy?

Mila: I've always liked that word

April: But he's my boss.

Ivy: From an HR point of view, that's not really a problem unless there is any question of a power imbalance. And I doubt nepotism is an issue in your current role.

Mila: It's handy having a CEO in the family.

April: I'm not going to do anything about it, anyway.

Mila: WHY NOT?

Ivy: WHY?

April: It's not the right time. I need to be single for a while. Right? Isn't that what you're supposed to do when your husband walks out on you?

Mila: I don't have a husband ;-)

Mila *did* have a very handsome, very successful boyfriend who adored her, however. Everyone knew they'd get married eventually.

April: Not helpful.

Mila: Sorry. Too soon?

Too soon to be teased about her situation?

April: No. I'm not curled up in the corner sobbing or anything.

She welcomed a bit of levity—she had right from the day that Evan had left her.

Plus, she was well past that now. Now she slept easily—no thoughts of Evan whatsoever. Working fourteen-hour days possibly also helped.

Ivy: I think being single for a while is a good idea.

Ivy was always good for keeping things on topic.

Mila: But you can still be single and do interesting things with an interesting man ;-) ;-)

Ivy: Exactly.

There was a long pause as her sisters clearly awaited her response.

This was not what she'd expected. She'd expected words of caution. Now the possibilities had short-circuited her brain.

Mila: April?

April: I don't know what to do.

Ivy: But you know WHO to do!

Mila: Ha-ha-ha!

April: Can you post some more photos of Nate?

Mila: Boo. You're no fun.

Ivy had taken the bait, though, and bombarded them with three adorable photos in quick succession. The conversation swiftly moved on, for which April was extremely grateful.

But that night it was Hugh Bennell who crowded her dreams.

April was almost finished for the day when Hugh opened the front door. The charity truck had just left, taking away the latest boxes full of donated things.

It had left the foyer almost empty, with only a neat

stack of flattened boxes near the door and the 'Hugh' box sitting on the bottom step of the grand stairway.

'Hello!' April said, smiling as he stepped inside. She hadn't seen him since the stripy blouse debacle, but had already determined her approach: regardless of her sisters' opinion, she was going to remain strictly professional.

Even *considering* another approach made her...

Well. It didn't matter. It was too soon after Evan, and Hugh was her boss. These were compelling supporting arguments for professionalism.

No matter how compelling Hugh himself might be, simply by walking through the glossy black door.

April had just sent him her summary email, but was doing a quick sweep-up of the dirt that the charity man had tracked inside before going home.

'Hi,' he said, shooting only the briefest glance in her direction before striding for his box. It was the first day since that afternoon in his basement that she'd had anything to add to it, and of course she'd let him know.

Hugh picked up the box in the swiftest of motions and then immediately headed down the hallway—which led through the kitchen, the utility room and then outside to the skip.

April had assumed he'd come and check the box after she'd gone for the day, so she wasn't really prepared for this.

'Wait!' she said, before she could stop herself.

He stopped, but didn't turn. 'Yes?' he asked. His tone was impatient.

She knew she shouldn't have said anything.

'Nothing—sorry,' she said.

There. Professional.

Then, somehow, she was jogging up the hallway. 'Wait...please.'

Again he stopped immediately at the sound of her voice.

This time he turned to face her.

She'd run up right behind him, so he was really close, with only the open box between them.

She reached inside. She'd found a lot of sentimental things across two boxes today: a large pile of ancient finger paintings and children's drawings—all labelled 'Hugh' with a date in the mid-nineteen-eighties—and all of his school reports, from pre-school through to Year Thirteen.

But it was some photos that she picked up now, in a messy pile she'd attempted to make neat. But that had been impossible with the collection of different-sized photos: some round-edged, others standard photo-sized, some cut out small and weathered, as if they'd been kept in someone's purse.

'These are from your first days of school,' she said.

Hugh didn't even look at them. He shrugged. 'I don't care.'

But he wasn't meeting her gaze, he was just looking—April thought—determinedly uninterested.

'I don't believe you.'

That got his attention.

'I beg your pardon?' he said, sounding as British as April had ever heard him.

'I don't believe you don't care,' she said, slowly and clearly. As if there was any chance he'd misunderstand.

His gaze was locked on hers now. 'I don't see how that matters.'

April fanned the photos out as if they were a deck of cards. 'Look,' she said, giving them a shake. 'These are photos of you in your school uniform. For each year there's a photo by yourself, with your school bag. And another with your mum. These are *special.*'

'They're not,' he said. He nodded at the box. 'Please put them back.'

April shook her head. 'No.'

'No?'

'No,' she said firmly, her gaze remaining steady.

It would seem she'd thrown her professionalism out of the window.

She'd get extra shifts at the supermarket if he fired her and the temp agency blacklisted her. Or clean toilets. Whatever. She just couldn't pretend that she agreed with this.

'You're making a mistake.'

His eyes narrowed. His voice was rough. 'You've got no idea what you're talking about.' He turned away from her and continued down the hallway. 'I'll just throw them out tomorrow.'

'Do you hate her?' April blurted out the words to his rapidly retreating back.

Faster than she'd thought possible he was back in front of her. *Right* in front of her. He'd dropped the box at some point and there was now no barrier between them.

His presence crowded her, but she didn't take a step back.

'*No!*' he said. Not loudly, but with bite. Then he blinked, and belatedly added, 'That is none of your business.'

His words were calm now, but—again—deliberately so.

'I know,' she said, because of course it was true. But she just couldn't stop. 'You know, I don't have any photos of myself with my mum like this,' she said conversationally. 'I know that because my sisters went through all Mum's old photos when I had my thirtieth birthday party, for one of those photoboard things.' She swallowed, ignoring Hugh's glower. 'I have a couple from my first day of school in Year One, but that's about it. And I have hardly any photos of myself as a kid with my mum. It was different twenty-five years ago—people didn't take as many photos. And it was usually Mum who *took* the photos anyway, rather than being in them.'

Hugh didn't say anything.

'I'd love photos of me like this with my mum. In fact I have more photos of me as a kid with my dad—again, because Mum was the photographer. And I don't even *like* him. But I love my mum.' She knew she was rambling, but didn't stop. 'So it's all backwards, really.'

'You don't like your dad?' Hugh asked.

April blinked. 'No. He left when I was five. I hardly saw him, growing up, and I have nothing to do with him now.'

Hugh nodded. 'My father did something similar,' he said. 'I never saw him again.'

He didn't elaborate further.

'That sucks,' she said.

His lips quirked. 'Yeah.'

'But your mum obviously loved you?'

She could see his jaw tense—but then relax. 'Yes,' he said. 'She did.'

'That's why she took all these photos.'

The tension was instantly back. 'The number of photos my mother took—and, trust me, within this house there are *thousands*—is not a reflection of how much she loved me, April. I'd still know she loved me if she hadn't taken even one. They're just *things.*'

April shook her head vigorously. 'No. They're not. They're memories. They're irreplaceable. What if you ever have kids? Won't you want to—?'

'I'm never having kids. And that is *definitely* none of your business.'

She didn't understand. She didn't understand any of this.

But he'd turned, retrieved the box from the floor. He faced her again, gesturing with the box for April to dump the photos inside.

But she couldn't. *She could not.*

'Why are you doing this?' she asked, still holding the photos tight.

For the first time the steady, unreadable gaze he'd trained on her began to slip. In his gaze—just briefly—there flashed emotion. Flashed pain.

'I don't have to explain anything to you, Ms Spencer. All I want is for you to empty this house. That's it. Empty the house. I don't require any commentary or concern or—'

'You want an empty house?' April interrupted, grasping forcefully on to a faint possibility.

He sighed with exasperation. 'Yes,' he said.

'Well, then,' she said, with a smile she could tell surprised him. 'I can work with that.'

'Work with what?' His expression was wary.

'Getting this stuff out of your mother's house.' A pause. 'Just not into a skip.'

'A storage unit solves nothing. This isn't about re-locating the hoard. I want it gone.'

Again she smiled, still disbelieving, and now she was certain she was right. 'You're the CEO of an international software company, right?' she said.

His eyes narrowed, but he didn't respond.

'So why didn't you think to just scan all this? You could even put it all in the cloud, so you don't even have a physical hard drive or anything left behind. It would be all gone, the house would be empty, and...'

And you won't do something you'll regret for the rest of your life.

But she didn't say that. Instinctively she knew she couldn't. She couldn't give him something to argue with—that he could refute with, *You've got no idea what you're talking about.*

Which would be true. Or *should* be true. But it wasn't. And, no matter how weird that was, and how little she knew about this man, she was certain she was right.

When she looked at Hugh Bennell—or at least when he *really* looked at *her*, and didn't obscure himself behind that indecipherable gaze—she saw so much emotion. So much...*more*. More than she'd see if he didn't care.

She was sure there were people out there who truly didn't care about photos and old school report cards and badly drawn houses with the sun a quarter crescent in the corner.

But one of those people was definitely not standing before her.

His gaze wasn't shuttered now. In fact she could sense he was formulating all matter of responses from disdain, to anger, to plans for her immediate dismissal.

As every second ticked by April began to realise that she was about to be fired.

But that was okay. At least she'd—

'That is a possibility,' he said suddenly. As if he was as surprised by his words as she was.

April grabbed on to them before he could change his mind. 'Awesome! I can even do it for you—it won't add much time…especially if you can get one of those scanners you can just feed a whole heap of stuff into at once. And maybe I can take photos of other stuff? Like if I find—'

'I'll organise the equipment you need.'

He stepped around April, carrying the box back into the foyer. He dropped it onto the bottom step and April added the pile of photos on top.

She wanted to say something, but couldn't work out what.

'Hugh—'

'It's late,' he said. 'You should go home. See you tomorrow.'

Then, just like that, he left.

CHAPTER SIX

THE NEXT AFTERNOON Hugh set up the scanner on the marble kitchen benchtop.

April was just finishing up the second reception room. He could hear the sound of the radio station she listened to above the rustle and thud of items being sorted.

When he'd interrupted her earlier to announce his presence she'd been singing—rather badly—to a song that he remembered being popular when he was back at high school.

She'd blushed when she'd seen him. The pinkening of her cheeks had been subtle—but then, he'd been looking for it, familiar now with the way she seemed to react to him.

He reacted too. As he always did around her. Even when she'd been standing before him, hands on hips, acting as self-designated saviour of old photos, evidence of his lack of artistic ability and irrelevant school reports.

Even then—as he'd struggled with the reality that the distance down that hallway to the skip had been traversed on feet that had felt weighted to the ground with lead—and *hated* himself for it—he'd reacted to her.

He'd reacted to the shape of her lips, to the way she managed to look so appealing while her hair escaped from its knot atop her head, and to the shape of her waist and hip as she leant against that broom...

And then he'd reacted to her imperious words, admiring her assertiveness even as he'd briefly hated her for delaying him. He'd needed to get that stuff out of the house. Quickly. Immediately. Before he succumbed to inertia like with the other box, which—while no longer on his coffee table—still taunted him from the back of the cupboard in his otherwise spotless spare room.

But then he had succumbed to April's alternative. At least temporarily.

If it keeps a good employee happy, then what's the problem? I can just delete it all once she finishes.

That was the conclusion he'd decided he'd come to.

He finished hooking up the scanner to the laptop he'd previously provided for April, then waited as the software was installed.

Footsteps drew his gaze away from the laptop screen.

April stood across from the kitchen bench, smiling again. *Sans* blush.

She looked confident and capable and in control—

as she always did in all but those moments between them he refused to let himself think about.

Again, questions flickered in his brain. Who was she, really? How had she ended up working here?

But that didn't matter. Their relationship was purely professional.

Really?

He mentally shook his head.

It was.

Belatedly he realised she was holding those damn photos.

'Shall we get started?' she asked.

This was when he should go. From her CV, he knew April was computer savvy—she'd work it out.

Instead, he held out his hand. 'Here, let me show you.'

They sat together, side by side at the kitchen bench, on pale wooden bar stools, scanning the photographs together.

They'd quickly fallen into a rhythm—Hugh fed the photos through the scanner and then April saved and filed them.

Initially she'd attempted to categorise the photos, but Hugh wouldn't have any of that. So April simply checked the quality of the scan, deleted any duplicates and saved them into one big messy folder.

Based on the decor of his flat, April would bet

that Hugh usually carefully curated his digital photos. He'd give them meaningful file names, he'd file them into sensibly organised folders, and he'd never keep anything blurry or any accidental photos of the sky.

But she got why he wasn't doing that today: he was telling himself he was just going to delete them all one day, anyway.

Was it weird that she could read an almost-stranger so easily? Especially when he was so deliberately attempting to reveal nothing.

Possibly.

Or possibly she was just spending too much time with young backpackers she had nothing in common with, pallets of groceries that needed to be stacked and walls of cardboard boxes? And now she was just constructing a connection with this man because in London she had no connections, and she wasn't very good at dealing with that?

That seemed more likely.

But, even so, she *liked* sitting this close to him. Liked the way their shoulders occasionally bumped, when they'd both act as if nothing had happened.

Or at least April did.

What was the reason she'd given her sisters for not...*doing* anything with Hugh?

Ah. That was right. She was still technically married.

And what would she do anyway? She'd had *one* boyfriend. *Ever.* She'd kissed one boy—slept with one man. Evan. That was it. Plus, Evan had pursued *her*. In the way of high school kids. With rumours that had spread through English Lit that Evan *liked* April. Like, *liked*, liked her.

She was ill-equipped to pursue a darkly handsome, intriguing, damaged man.

But what if she turned to him? Right now? And said his name? Softly...the way she really wanted too? And what if he kissed her? How would his lips feel against hers? What would it be like to kiss another man? To be pressed up tight against another man...?

'April?'

She jumped, making her bar stool wobble.

'You okay?'

She put her hands on the benchtop to steady herself. 'Yes, of course.'

He looked at her curiously. Not anything like the way he had that day of the stripy top.

Another of those damn blushes heated her cheeks. It was ridiculous—she was never normally one to blush.

'In my first day-at-school photos, from Year One, I'm always with my sisters. I'm the middle child. That means I'm supposed to have issues, right?'

She was rambling—needing to fill the tense silence. In addition to never blushing, she *never* rambled. She had sparkling, meaningless conversation down to an art—she'd been to enough charity functions/opening nights/award galas to learn how to speak to *anyone*. Intelligently, even.

Not with Hugh.

'My big sister is a typical first child. *Such* an overachiever. I get exhausted just thinking about all she does. Although my baby sister has never really felt like the baby. She's kind of wise beyond her years—she always has been. But that fits with something I read about third-born children—they're supposed to be risk-takers, and creative, which totally fits her.'

She paused, but couldn't stop.

'You know what middle children are supposed to be? Like, their defining characteristic? *Peacemakers*. I mean, come on? How boring is *that*?'

She was staring at the laptop screen and all the photos of cherubic child-sized Hugh.

'You're not boring,' he said.

April blinked, hardly believing he'd been paying attention.

'Thank you,' she said. She rotated the latest photo on the screen and dragged it over to the folder she'd created.

'I can see the peacemaker thing, too. Just not when it comes to my old school photos.'

April grinned. 'Nope,' she said. 'Especially when

I wish *I* had photos like this. My mum worked really hard when we were growing up. She was often already at work when it was time for us to go to school.'

'What did she do?' Hugh asked.

She swallowed. 'She worked in an office in the city,' she said vaguely. *As CEO of Australia's largest mining company.* The words remained unsaid.

Thankfully, Hugh just nodded. 'My mum had lots of different jobs when I was growing up. We didn't have a lot of money, so she often juggled a couple of jobs—you know, waitressing, receptionist...she even stacked shelves at a supermarket for a while, when I was old enough to be alone for a few hours at night.'

This was the longest conversation they'd ever had.

'*I* do that!' April exclaimed. 'After I get home from this job.'

'Really?' he asked. 'Why?'

April shrugged. 'So I can get out of the awful shared house I live in in Shoreditch.'

His gaze flicked over her—ever so quickly. April ignored the way her body shivered.

'Aren't you a bit old to live in a shared house?'

She narrowed her eyes in mock affront. 'Well, yeah,' she said. 'I'm thirty-two. But I made some dumb decisions with a credit card and I need to pay it off.'

She was choosing her words carefully, keen to keep everything she told him truthful, even if she wasn't being truly honest with him.

But then, her family's billions really shouldn't be relevant. That, after all, was the whole point of this London 'adventure'. Even if it *had* made a dodgy flatshare detour.

'What kind of dumb decisions?' he asked.

The question surprised her. She hadn't expected him to be interested. 'Clothes. Eating out. Rent I couldn't afford. No job. That kind of thing.'

He nodded. 'When I first moved out of home I rented this ridiculous place in Camden. It was way bigger than what a brand-new graduate needed, and my mum thought I was nuts.'

'So you racked up lots of debt, too?'

'No. I'd just sold a piece of software I'd developed for detecting plagiarism in uni assignments for two hundred and fifty thousand pounds, so the rent wasn't a problem,' Hugh replied. 'But I did move out because all that space was really echoey.'

April laughed out loud.

'And—let me guess—you didn't move into a shared house?'

His lips quirked upwards. 'No. I can't think of anything worse.'

'You *do* realise your story has nothing in common with mine, right?'

He shrugged. 'Hey, we both made poor housing choices.'

'Nope. No comparison. One of my housemates inexplicably collects every hair that falls out of her head in the shower. Like, in a little container that she leaves on the windowsill. I...'

'I'll pay off all your credit card debt if you stop your sentimental junk crusade.'

It wasn't a throwaway line. He said it with deadly seriousness.

April tilted her head as she studied him. 'I know—and you know—that if you really wanted this stuff gone it would already be gone. Some random Aussie girl nagging you about it wouldn't make any difference.'

He slid off his stool, then walked around to the other side of the kitchen bench. She watched as he filled the kettle, then plonked it without much care onto its base. But he didn't flick the lever that would turn it on.

He grabbed April's mug from the sink, and another from the overhead cupboard, then put both cups side by side, near the stone-cold kettle.

'Do you want to talk about it?' she asked. She could only guess at whatever was swirling about in his brain. His attention was seemingly focused on the marble swirls of the benchtop.

His head shot up and their gazes locked.

'*No.*'

'Cool,' April said with a shrug. 'I don't need to know.'

Although she realised she *wanted* to know. Really wanted to.

April slid off her stool, too. She skirted around the bench, terribly aware of Hugh's gaze following her. She didn't *quite* meet his gaze. She couldn't. Even as thoughts of discovering what was really going on in Hugh's head zipped through her mind, other thoughts distracted her. About discovering how Hugh might feel if his lovely, strong body— hot as hell, even in jeans and jumper—was pressed against hers. If, say, he kissed her against the pantry door just beside him...

Stop.

This was Ivy and Mila's influence, scrambling her common sense. It wasn't how she really felt. She'd *never* felt like this.

She reached past him, incredibly careful not to brush against him, and switched on the kettle.

She sensed rather than saw him smile—her gaze was on the kettle, not him.

'Let me help you,' she said. 'Stop trying to convince yourself you want something you don't actually want. At all. Stop pretending.'

Too late, she realised the error of her 'help him with the kettle the way she'd help him with his stuff' metaphor. She'd ended up less than a foot away from him.

Or maybe it hadn't been an error at all.

'Okay,' he said. His voice was deep. Velvety.

April looked up and their gazes locked.

It was like the stripy blouse moment all over again. But more, even.

She was suddenly unbelievably aware of her own breathing—the rise and fall of her chest was shallow, fast. And the way her belly clenched, the way her nails were digging into her palms to prevent herself from touching him.

'I'll stop pretending,' he said.

His gaze slid to her lips.

She closed her eyes. She had to, or she couldn't think.

The way Hugh was looking at her...

'April...?' he said, so soft.

Was that his breath against her lips? Had he moved closer so he could kiss her?

She refused to find out.

Instead, she stepped away. Two steps...three.

'Good!' she said. 'Great! Let's make time to go through the stuff I find each couple of days, okay?'

Hugh wasn't thinking about the boxes. 'What?'

April nodded sharply. 'Okay, I can finish up here. Thanks for your help.'

He was gone a minute later—just as the kettle whistled to say that it had boiled.

Later, as she walked to the supermarket, all rugged up in scarf and coat, Hugh's words echoed in her brain.

I'll stop pretending.

But *she* wouldn't stop pretending. She couldn't.

For now she was April Spencer, not April Molyneux.

The thing was she had no idea what was pretend any more.

Hugh sat at his desk, typing a message to an old friend from university.

Ryan had completed the same computer science qualification that Hugh had, although he'd made his money in a completely different field—internet dating. Ryan's innovative compatibility matching algorithm had been game-changing at the time. But his friend had long since sold the empire he'd built, and now ran an extremely discreet, exclusive online dating agency, using a new—Ryan said better—matching algorithm.

This had come in handy for Hugh.

Ryan's system was cutting-edge, and Hugh honestly couldn't fault it. He'd liked every woman he'd met through Ryan's system—even if he hadn't been attracted to them all. Or them to him.

After all—there still wasn't an app that could guarantee that.

He didn't date often, but when he did he was very specific. He liked to meet at quiet, private restaurants where it was easy to converse without distraction. He'd go to the movies, or to a show. He didn't go to bars or pubs—there was too little order and too many people talking. He couldn't think.

If things went well, after a few dates he might sleep over at his date's place. But he never lingered long the morning after. Or stayed for breakfast.

Usually, at some point later, he'd be invited to a party, or to a family event.

He always said no.

At such events he would become 'the boyfriend'. And he didn't want that.

Understandably, usually things ended then.

A couple of times he'd met women equally happy to avoid a relationship. Those arrangements had lasted longer, until eventually they'd run their course too.

Of course he was always clear that he wasn't after a relationship, and he was never matched with anybody who specifically wanted to settle down. However, it would seem that the 'wanting a relationship' and 'not wanting a relationship' continuum was not linear. And everyone's definition of where they stood along that line varied. Wildly.

So a woman who started off not wanting a relationship might actually want a bit of clarity around her relationship with Hugh. Or an agreement of exclusivity.

And exclusivity, to Hugh, was an indicator of a relationship—not that he had ever dated more than one woman at once, however casually.

So at that point he was out.

He got it that he was weird when it came to relationships. Women always eventually asked him about his stance. But it wasn't easy for him to define.

He knew, intellectually, that it originated from his mother's serial dating. She had been quite openly on a quest to find her Mr Right after the disappearance of his deadbeat father. He'd become used to the cycle of hope and despair that each new boyfriend would bring, and he'd decided he had no wish to experience that for himself.

But—and this had been his original theory—the risk of a relationship ending in despair was surely reduced if you approached dating with comprehensive data on your side. If you were matched appropriately—your values, your interests, your goals—then surely you minimised risk.

And this, in his experience, was true. He had never experienced the euphoric highs or the devastating lows of his mother's relationships. When he dated it was…*uncomplicated.*

But that was where his stance on relationships became much more about *him*. Because, despite all this data-matching and uncomplicated dating, he still didn't want a relationship.

It was a visceral thing. When he woke up in a woman's bed—he never invited them to *his* place— his urge to leave was not dissimilar from the way the bloody boxes that filled his mother's house made him feel.

Trapped.

It all came back to the same thing: to Hugh, relationships were clutter.

Ryan: I'll send you the link to our latest questionnaire—we've tweaked things a little so you'll need to answer a few more compatibility questions.

Hugh: No problem.

Ryan: Then the system will automatically send you a shortlist. Same as always—if the women you say yes for also say yes then you're set.

Hugh: Great. Thanks.

But it was weird… He'd been keen to talk to Ryan, but now he was losing enthusiasm. He'd been so sure that it was the six or more months since his last date that had triggered his interest in April. And today he'd almost kissed her.

Hugh: What's your current success rate with your matching algorithm?

Ryan wouldn't need time to look this up—he knew his company inside out.

Ryan: Almost one hundred per cent. We rarely have a customer receive no matches.

That wasn't what Hugh had meant.

Hugh: So one hundred per cent go on at least one date?

Ryan: Yes. And over ninety per cent of users rate their first date experience with a score of eight or above. We're very proud of that stat.

Hugh: Second date?

Ryan: We don't track activity beyond the first date.

Hugh: Long-term relationships? Engagements? Marriages?

Ryan: Lots. There are many testimonials available.

He pasted a link, but Hugh didn't click on it.

Hugh: Percentages?

Ryan: We don't have that data.

Hugh: Could you guess?

He could just imagine Ryan sighing at his laptop screen.

Ryan: Low. Easily under ten per cent. Under five per cent, probably. Which makes sense when you consider that each user gets matched with multiple people. But anyway our job is the introduction. The rest is up to the couple. But, mate, why the interest? Do we need to update your profile to 'Seeking a long-term relationship'?

Hugh: No. Just—

He stopped typing.
Just *what*?
Why was he suddenly questioning the method he'd been following for ten years? Especially when he'd contacted Ryan today to follow that exact method again. Nothing different. No changes.
He finished the sentence:

Hugh: No. Just wondering.

If Ryan had been a close friend—the kind of mate who knew when you were talking out of your backside—he would've questioned that. But he wasn't a close friend. Hugh didn't have close friends. The habits of his childhood—of keeping people at a distance, and certainly away from his home—had never abated.

Hugh asked Ryan a few more questions—just being social now. About his new house, his new baby...

After several baby photos, Ryan wrote: We should catch up for a beer. Somewhere quiet, of course.

Hugh: Sure.

And maybe they *would* organise it. But, in reality, ninety-five per cent of their friendship was conducted via video-conference or instant message. And that suited Hugh just fine.

Later, he answered the new compatibility questions.

He hesitated before submitting them.

Why?

Because his subconscious was cluttered with thoughts of April Spencer.

Particularly the way she'd looked at him that afternoon in the kitchen. Particularly the way her lips had parted when she'd closed her eyes.

But Ryan's algorithm would never match him with April.

April was vivacious and definitely sociable. She had an easy sunniness to her—he found it difficult to imagine that many people would dislike April. He imagined her surrounded by an ever-expand-ing horde of friends and family, living somewhere eclectic and noisy.

While he— Well, he had a handful of friends like Ryan. A handful he felt no need to expand. No family.

She was a traveller...an adventurer. She must be to be her age and working at this job in London. Meanwhile, he'd lived nowhere but North London. And he rarely travelled—save for those essential meetings when he'd first expanded his company internationally. Now he insisted all such meetings took place via video-conference.

He was intensely private, and unused to having his decisions questioned.

She questioned him boldly, and she'd told him about her family and her absent father without the slightest hesitation.

And somehow he'd revealed more to her than to anyone he could remember.

So, no, they wouldn't have been matched.

Apart from the added complication of her working for him, their obvious incompatibility could not be ignored.

He was attracted to her—that was inarguably apparent. She was beautiful. It was natural, but it didn't mean anything. April Spencer was all complications. He didn't *do* complicated.

What he needed was a date with a woman who

knew exactly what he was offering and vice versa. And who was like him: quiet, private, solitary. No ambiguity. No confusion. Just harmless, uncomplicated fun.

He clicked '*Submit*'.

A minute later he received an email confirmation that his responses had been received.

Now he just needed to wait to be matched.

CHAPTER SEVEN

APRIL SAT CROSS-LEGGED in bed. It was Sunday, and her roommate had headed out for brunch, taking advantage of an unseasonably warm winter's day.

Loving my new nails! So pretty. What's your go-to shade for summer? #diymanicure #mint #glam #THEnailpolish

April studied her nails after she'd scheduled her post to appear at about this time the next day, Perth time—eight hours away. She'd painted them the lovely minty green that THE had supplied, along with their generous Molyneux Foundation donation. Her assistant, Carly, had priority-mailed the bottle overnight all the way to London—at a ridiculous cost that April planned to pay back to the Molyneux Foundation. But it had had to be done.

It was getting increasingly complicated as each week went by to be both April Molyneux and April Spencer. To be truthful, she hadn't really planned this far ahead, and while her absences at social events had so far been attributed to her marriage breakdown, that excuse wouldn't last for ever.

So far her Instagram account had supported the narrative of a fragile divorcee-to-be with carefully curated images. Yesterday she'd posted one of the photos she'd taken with Carly just before she'd flown to London. In that image—despite her blow-dried hair and designer-sponsored dress, apparently going for dinner with her sisters—she fitted the brief well.

She *had* looked fragile. Because she had been.

When that photo had been taken she'd been barely a month on from that devastating evening at the beach.

At the time, April hadn't seen it. Maybe because she'd become used to seeing herself like that in the mirror: her gaze flat, her smile not quite convincing.

She'd been wearing heaps of make-up to hide the shadows beneath her eyes, to give colour to her cheeks. Without it she'd looked like death. And not in an edgy, model-like way. But really crap. Like, *my husband has just left me* crap.

She didn't, she realised, look like that now.

When had that happened?

She dismissed the thought. It was more important that it had—that Evan and all he represented no longer dominated her psyche.

She wiggled her nails, liking the way the sun that poured through the windows made them sparkle.

She'd flung open the curtains both for better light for her photos and to revel in experiencing actual sun in London.

Her sponsors were also tricky. But Carly was doing well: scheduling long into the future, where possible, and being creative with everything else. After all, it wasn't essential that April appeared in every photo. She'd even roped Mila into one—with her sister admirably hamming up her mock-serious pose as she'd modelled long strands of stunning Broome pearls. This nail polish was the first product that had definitely required April to model it. It had been specified by the company, and her hands had featured in too many photos to risk that an eagle-eyed follower wouldn't notice a substitution. Not that she would have considered it anyway...

But April knew that this couldn't continue for ever.

The thing was, she'd assumed she'd have everything worked out already.

She'd imagined writing an inspirational post—maybe at her desk at her Fabulous Job In London. She'd talk about overcoming life's challenges. About realising that she needed to stand on her own two feet and chase her dreams.

And she'd write that she'd done it all by herself, without using her family name to leap to the front of the queue.

Ugh.

That would've been rather sickening, wouldn't it? As if someone as privileged as her was in any position to present herself as poster girl for grit and determination.

Well, she certainly couldn't post a little snapshot of her life right now. It had been an effort to photograph her hands without accidentally including a glimpse of the peeling walls, or the cheap laminate floor, or the battered beds and bedside tables. She'd actually ended up using a pretty plum velvet cushion she'd retrieved from one of Hugh's 'donate' boxes to lay her manicured fingers artistically across—after asking permission from Hugh via email, of course.

Take anything you want, he'd said.

Hugh...

He hadn't come up to the main house on Friday. There'd been no need with nothing for him to sort through.

Which was for the best, she'd told herself. Firmly.

And yet her realisation that there was no need for her to see Hugh that day had been tinged with both relief and disappointment.

She'd finished up in the front reception room and was now up the stairs, working on the front guest bedroom. It wasn't quite as packed with boxes as the first two rooms, although it was definitely a marginal thing. The first few boxes had been full of beautiful manchester—a word she'd discovered was actually a term for bedlinen used only in Australia and New Zealand when she'd provided her summary to Hugh and subsequently confused him.

See? She was learning so much from her move to London. April grinned. Just not exactly what she'd expected.

Sitting, as she was, on the cheapest doona—*duvet*, she'd learnt, in the UK—she'd been able to find at her local supermarket, she questioned her decision not to take one of the beautiful, soft vintage white linen covers she'd found on Friday.

But she couldn't. As hard as she was trying to live as if she wasn't, she *was* an heiress—with a mammoth trust fund. Someone shopping at the local charity shop deserved an expensive doona cover far more than she did.

What was she doing?

In London? Living in this dodgy shared house? Working for Hugh?

Based on her current progress, in another month she would have paid off her credit card. Only another month of two jobs, rice, beans, two-minute noodles and tins of soup.

And then what?

Would she quit her night job? Start applying for jobs back in her own field—or at least her field of study? Eventually move out of this place to some place on her own?

She didn't know.

If she did that she'd definitely need to shut down her social media profiles. There was no way she could continue to use them for the Molyneux Foundation all the way over here.

The idea felt unexpectedly uncomfortable.

Because, surely, her social media profile represented all that had been excessive in her life? Shouldn't she be glad to be rid of it? Glad that she'd be leaving that version of herself behind?

But...

It also represented how successful she'd been—how well she'd connected with her followers and how seamlessly she'd incorporated her sponsors. It represented how much money she'd raised for the foundation by being social media savvy and putting all that Molyneux privilege to good use.

She had over a million followers, and she'd worked hard for every single one of them.

It was only logical reasoning to suppose that those followers were unlikely to care about her new, unglamorous life, but that didn't make the idea of deleting her accounts seem any more appealing.

She wasn't entirely sure what it said about her, but she wasn't ready to give her followers up.

Not yet, anyway.

* * *

On Tuesday, April found more photos to add to the 'Hugh' box.

This time it was a bunch of birthday photos, all stuffed into a large white envelope that had become deeply creased and soft with years of handling.

She carried it downstairs to the kitchen, leaving it on the kitchen bench while she turned on the kettle for her morning tea break.

The photos she'd scanned with Hugh still remained in the 'Hugh' box, atop the benchtop. They hadn't worked out the finer details after he'd left so abruptly, and she hadn't seen him since. Was she supposed to keep on scanning the photos she found? Or would he? Or would he not even bother now and just keep the photos…?

She should just put them into the box and let Hugh decide.

Instead she found herself pulling up one of the bar stools and settling down with both her coffee and the envelope before her.

Even as she slid the photos out she questioned what she was doing. There was no need to *look* at the photos, really. And so to do so felt…not quite right. But that was silly, really. It was her *job*, after all, to go through everything in this house. That was what she was doing.

And so she did look.

Like the images from Hugh's first days at school, these birthday shots were across all of Hugh's birthdays. The envelope was chock-full of them—several from every year. The classic 'blowing out the candles' shot, breakfast in bed with unwrapped presents and always a photo of Hugh with his mum. The very early ones also featured his father.

His mum, of course, had been stunning. April had thought so when she'd first seen her in those school photos. She'd had dark hair and eyes, like Hugh, but her face had been rounder and her eyes and lips had looked as if they always smiled, not just in photos. She'd worn her long hair mostly loose, and had alternated year to year from having a fringe and growing it out.

These photos were different from the school ones, though, which had all been taken outside Hugh's kindergarten or primary school. These were taken indoors. And not all in *this* house, which surprised April.

For some reason she'd assumed this was the house where Hugh had grown up, but the photos showed she was wrong. Silly of her, really, given she'd known his mum hadn't had much money, and Islington was decidedly posh.

April took a sip from her coffee, and then shuffled back to the beginning again.

Outside, it had started raining, and the occasional fat droplet slapped against the kitchen window.

The first photo had a chubby Hugh sitting on his mother's lap, reaching out with both hands for a birthday cake in the shape of a lime-green number one. Standing at his mother's shoulder was—April assumed—his father. A tall man, but narrower in the shoulders than Hugh, he had dark blond hair. He was handsome, but his smile looked uncomfortable.

They sat at a dining table with a mid-nineteen-eighties swirly beige laminate top. Behind them was a sideboard with shelving above it, neatly filled with books, trinkets and brass-framed photographs.

For Hugh's second birthday the cake photo was again taken at the same table. This time Hugh looked as if he was deliberately avoiding the camera, his gaze focused on something out of the picture. Again, he was with his mum and dad. There were more things now, on the shelves behind Hugh and his parents: more brass-framed photographs, more books. But still neat.

For his third birthday Hugh had had a cake in the shape of a lion, with skinny, long pieces of liquorice creating its eyes, nose and whiskers. There was no dad in this one, and while the table and sideboard were still the same the paint on the walls was now blue, not beige. There was less on the shelves—only a few photos. A new house? Or new paint?

April checked the other photos from his third birthday—yes, definitely a new house. His breakfast in bed was no longer beside a lovely double sash window, but instead one with a cheap-looking frame, probably aluminium.

His mum, though, still smiled her luminous smile.

When Hugh had turned four, the birthday parties had clearly begun.

There was Hugh playing pass the parcel, sitting on top of an oriental-style rug with his friends. Or playing pin the tail on the donkey. This photo was a wider shot, showing Hugh from the side, blindfolded and with his arm outstretched. Beyond him was a small kitchen, where a row of parents stood, some observing their kids, others chatting to each other.

The room was very neat, the kitchen bench clear but for trays of party food. In fact in all these early photos every room was tidy. April knew that careful angle selection could make the messiest room appear tidy, but she didn't believe that was the case here. There wasn't one cardboard box, or any pile of useless random things to put inside one, anywhere to be seen.

When had it started?

April flipped ahead through the photos, trying to work it out.

In the end it was that sideboard behind the dining table that told the story.

In front of that blue-painted wall it gained items year on year. At first neatly. More books, more photos, more trinkets, a small vase, a snow globe. But each item had definitely been carefully placed.

By the time Hugh had reached age seven the shelves were stuffed full. So many books jammed in horizontally and vertically. Photos in mismatched frames along the top. A few more trinkets...fat ivory candles. A carved wooden horse.

But still neat. *Organised* chaos.

By Hugh's ninth birthday it was just chaos.

Books were randomly stacked with pages outwards. The vase had been knocked over and damaged, but it still remained on its side in multiple pieces. Paper had now appeared on the shelves: envelopes with plastic windows, sheets of paperwork... piles of magazines.

In the background of a blurry photo of kids dancing—musical statues?—April spotted a cardboard box. Just one. Beside it was a stack of newspapers, and beside that a stack of books.

But in the photo of Hugh and his mum together she was still smiling. Her hair was still lovely, her eyes sparkling. Hugh was smiling too, looking up at his mum.

April's throat felt tight and prickly.

It seemed impossible, given she'd now spent weeks surrounded by the hoard, but until now she hadn't really thought about the actual compulsive hoarding that must have occurred for this house to be in this state.

Maybe because the house was very neat—for a house full of boxes. And April associated hoarding with those unfortunate people you saw on television documentaries, with rotting food and mountains of rubbish. Vermin. This place wasn't like that.

But that didn't mean accumulating all this junk was normal.

April went back to the photos. For Hugh's tenth birthday there had been no party. Possibly he just hadn't wanted to have one, but April doubted it.

There weren't any party photos the year after, or any of the years after that.

Instead it was just pictures of Hugh and his mum and—in the background—more and more boxes...

'Boxes suck as party decorations.'

Hugh's voice made April jump.

Her stool wobbled dramatically, and his hand landed firmly at her waist, steadying her.

She was wearing a chunky knitted jumper with a wide neck. The wool was soft against his fingers and the shape of her waist a perfect fit against his palm. But he made sure his hand dropped away the instant the chair was still.

A moment after that April practically leapt from her seat, turning to face him.

'I didn't hear you,' she said, unnecessarily.

Her gaze roamed over him—just briefly. He was wearing his normal uniform of sorts: jeans, T-shirt, hoodie, trainers. Completely unremarkable.

And yet he sensed April's appreciation. She liked how he looked.

Although hadn't he known that since he'd helped her out of that stripy top? He'd certainly appreciated how April looked from the moment he'd first seen her.

Today was no different.

She wore light-washed jeans, and her jumper was pale lemon, oversized and slouchy, revealing much of her golden shoulders and a thin silver chain at her neck. Her dark hair was scraped back from her face in a high ponytail. It was neater than normal—probably because it was early in the day, and all those rogue strands hadn't had the opportunity to escape.

He gave himself a mental shake. It wasn't important. Wasn't he supposed to be annoyed with her?

That was what he'd meant to do when he'd walked into the kitchen to find April so absorbed in those photos that she hadn't heard his approach. He'd meant to ask her, *What the hell are you doing?*

Although, he reflected, that *would* have been a dumb question.

She was looking at photos. *Duh.*

But why? There was no need any more. The photos were *his* responsibility now. And something about having her look through them felt…almost intimate. Crazy when a few days ago she'd done the same thing with his school photos and he hadn't cared.

Or at least hadn't *let* himself care. He'd still been telling himself the photos were worthless and meaningless to him, after all.

But that hadn't been true.

So maybe that was why his instinctive reaction was anger—anger that she'd been looking at images he now accepted meant something to him. Just what they meant he could work out later. They were his, and they were private photos. None of her business.

But by the time he'd gone to speak he hadn't been angry at all.

Boxes suck as party decorations.

'You stopped having birthday parties,' April said, reading his mind.

'Yeah,' Hugh said.

He stepped closer to the bench, picking up a bundle of the photos she'd been studying with such concentration. He'd dump them in the box to take down to his flat. He would go through the photos later. It had been nice of April to offer to help him, but it wasn't necessary.

'I didn't notice at first,' he said. 'You know...all the clutter, I mean. I was a kid. It was just my house. When I was old enough to tidy I kept my room pretty neat, but the rest of the house... I don't know. Like I said, it was just my house.'

Hugh hadn't intended to continue the conversation. *At all.* And yet—he continued.

'The other kids didn't notice either. Why would they? Their parents may have, but I wouldn't have known, and Mum never would've cared.'

'Really?' April asked with raised eyebrows.

Hugh shook his head. 'No. At first it wasn't that bad, and my mum had always been pretty forthright about people accepting each other for who they were. She figured if the house was a bit untidy what was the big deal?'

'But you didn't like it?'

'No,' he said. 'And it just got worse. And as kids get older they notice things. I had a friend over one day after school, before it got really bad, and he had a box fall on him while we were playing. He was fine, but I remember his mum talking to my mum in this really low, concerned voice, asking if she was okay and if she'd like some help. My mum didn't like that. She laughed, I remember, and said she'd just had a busy week and really needed to get all the stuff to the charity shop.'

He was flipping through the photos, but not looking at them.

'That was a lie. I knew she was never going to do that. Although I suppose maybe she was telling herself that she would one day. I don't know. But—anyway—my mum never lied. Ever. And that combined with the other mum obviously thinking something was wrong... Well, then I knew something was wrong. So I didn't have anyone over again.'

April hadn't moved from where she stood. She just watched him, letting him speak.

'Things got worse after that. Mum was always really sociable. I remember when I was really little that she'd have these elaborate dinner parties where she'd always try something fancy out of this fat hardcover cookbook she'd get from the library. But they stopped, too. She'd still go out and see her friends—we had a nice neighbour and I'd go and stay with her and watch TV—but the house was just for us. Us and the damn boxes.'

'That must have been hard,' April said.

Her words were soft. Kind. That was the *last* thing he wanted. Kindness. Pity. He didn't know her. Why was he telling her this?

'I was fine,' he said, his words hard-edged. 'I managed.'

She stepped close to him now and reached out her hand, resting it just below his elbow.

Instinctively he shook his arm free. 'What are you doing?'

She looked surprised—at her action or his, he couldn't be sure.

April swallowed. 'Sorry. I...' There was a pause, then she straightened her shoulders. 'I wanted to touch you,' she said. 'I thought it might help.'

He shook his head. 'It was a long time ago,' he said. 'I'm fine.'

'A long time ago?' she prompted, her forehead wrinkled.

Hugh ran a hand through his hair. 'I mean since I had to live like that. Mum—' He hadn't intended to explain, but he couldn't stop himself. 'When she met Len I was in the Lower Sixth, and she got better. She got the help she needed—did this cognitive behavioural therapy stuff, got in a professional organiser—and then, when she married Len, we moved here. She was good for a long time. It only started again when Len died, and—honestly—I did all I could. *Everything* I could think of to stop it happening again, to stop her filling the emptiness she felt after my father left and Len died with *stuff*. Objects she could cling on to for ever, that would never leave her—'

Her hand was on his arm again. His gaze shot downwards, staring at it. Immediately she removed her touch.

'I'm sorry, I—'

'It's okay,' he said. 'I don't mind. It felt good.'

She placed her hand on his arm again.

Her touch through the fabric of his hoodie was light against his skin. Her fingers didn't grip…they were just there.

'I'm a hugger,' April explained, her gaze also trained on her hand. 'I can't help it. I hug everybody. Happy, sad, indifferent. Hug, hug, hug.' She sighed. 'It's sucked, really, not having anyone to hug since I've been in London.'

'You want a hug?' he asked, confused.

Her head shot up and she grinned. 'No!' she said. 'I was just explaining.' She nodded at their hands. 'The touching thing. Because I'm guessing you're not a hugger.'

A rough laugh burst from his throat. 'No,' he said. 'I'm not a hugger.'

Her lips curved upwards again. 'I thought so.'

He rarely touched anyone except by accident. When would he? He had no family. A handful of friends. He worked remotely. He was resolutely single. And when he dated touch was about sex. Not this—not reassurance or comfort. This was touch without expectations.

It should be strange, really, to find comfort in the touch of a woman he was attracted to. The few times they'd touched before had been fleeting, but charged with electricity. And, yes, that current was still there. Of course it was.

But what she was offering was straightforward: her touch was simply to help him calm his thoughts and to acknowledge the uncomfortable memories he'd just shared.

It was working, too.

His gaze drifted from her hand to the photos he still grasped. On top was a photo taken of him in bed the morning of his tenth birthday. He'd just unwrapped his present: a large toy robot that he'd coveted for months. His mum had used the timer on her camera, propping it on his dresser, and she sat beside him, her arm around him, his superhero pillows askew behind them.

He and his mum were both smiling in the photo, and Hugh smiled now. A proper smile at a happy memory.

'Thank you,' he said.

For making him keep the photographs. For listening.

'My pleasure,' said April.

Then she squeezed his arm and her touch fell away.

'Wait,' he said.

CHAPTER EIGHT

HUGH'S VOICE WAS LOW. Different from before.

April went still. Her hand fell back against her thigh, already missing his warmth.

He stepped towards her, close enough that she needed to tilt her chin up, just slightly, to meet his gaze.

He studied her intently. 'Why did you leave behind all the people you used to hug?' he asked.

Her gaze wavered.

She put on a smile. 'Early midlife crisis,' she said. Best to keep it simple.

'No,' he said. 'Why are you here? Why are you working for me?'

She shrugged. 'I told you the other day. Credit card debt.'

He looked her dead in the eye. 'I don't believe you.'

Ah. He was echoing her own words…the way she'd been challenging him.

She hadn't expected the tables to turn.

She twisted her fingers in the too-long sleeves of

her jumper...the fabric was all nubbly beneath her fingertips.

She wasn't used to being secretive. She did, after all, document her life for millions of strangers. But this was different.

Hugh didn't talk the way he just had about his past very often. Ever, maybe. April knew that—was sure of it. She understood what he'd revealed to her. How big a deal it was for him. So he deserved her honesty—she knew that.

But her reticence wasn't just about hiding April Molyneux from a man who thought her to be April Spencer—it was more than that. There was something about Hugh—something between them that was just so different. So intense.

Until today they'd only teased the very edges of that intensity, and neither had taken it any further.

They'd both resisted temptation. The temptation to touch. To kiss.

Right now—with these questions, this conversation—it wasn't as primal as before, although all that continued to simmer below the surface. But it was still a connection. And it still felt raw. As if sharing any part of herself, even her past, was only the start of a slippery slope.

It would lead to more. Much more.

And that was as tempting as it was frightening.

Frightening?

What was she scared of?

She didn't answer her own question. It didn't matter. Because she hadn't come all the way to London to be scared of anything.

'My husband left me,' she said.

Silence.

She'd expected him to recoil. Because surely *this* wasn't the conversation Hugh Bennell wanted to have with her?

Instead, he nodded. 'Are you okay?' he asked simply.

She smiled. Genuinely this time. 'Yes,' she said with confidence. 'Now. Sucked for a bit, though.'

He smiled too.

'I needed a change. So here I am. Unpacking your boxes and stacking supermarket shelves. Trust me, it's not as glamorous a midlife crisis as I'd expected.'

'What happened?' he asked. Gently.

'We fell out of love,' she said. 'Him first, but me too. I just hadn't realised it. So I'm okay. Not heartbroken or anything. But it was still sad.'

'Not heartbroken?' he prompted.

Her gaze had travelled downwards, along his jaw and chin. Now it flew upwards, locking with his.

'What do *you* think?' she asked.

Her gaze was heated. Hot. Deliberately so.

Nope. Definitely not scared any more.

'No,' he said, his voice deliciously low. 'I don't think you are.'

And just like that weeks of tension, of attraction, of *connection* were just—*there*. No glancing away, no changing the subject, no pretending it didn't exist.

It was *there*. Unequivocally.

Oh, God.

His eyes were dark, and intensely focused on her. He'd moved closer again, so that only centimetres separated them, and there was no question about what he wanted to do next.

He leant closer. Close enough that his breath was hot against her cheek and then her ear.

'I want to kiss you,' he said, and the low rawness of his voice made her shiver.

How did he know? April thought. That she needed that? That she needed a moment? That despite the crackling tension between them doubts still tugged at her?

Could she trust her instincts after what had happened to her marriage? She'd got it all so very wrong. And, even more than that, could she actually kiss another man?

It had been so long—so very, very long...

'Kiss me,' she said, because she couldn't wait another moment.

Although it turned out she had to.

His lips were at her ear, and he didn't move them

far. Instead he pressed his mouth to the sensitive skin of her neck, at the edge of her jaw. Suddenly her knees were like jelly, but strong hands at her waist steadied her.

The sensation of his lips against her neck and his hands against her body was *so good*, and April's eyes slid shut as a sigh escaped from her mouth.

Her fingers untangled themselves from the sleeves of her jumper and reached for Hugh blindly, hitting the solid wall of his stomach and sliding up and around to the breadth of his back.

Hugh dotted her jaw with kisses that were firm but soft. And glorious. But not even close to enough. More than almost anything, she wanted to turn her head to meet his mouth with hers—but she didn't. Because, even more than she wanted that, she wanted this anticipation to last for ever. This promise of Hugh's kiss that, she realised, had been growing from the moment they'd met.

But he was definitely going to kiss her now—this mysterious man who was so different to anyone she'd ever met—and the wonder of that she wanted to hold on to. Just a few seconds longer.

By the time his mouth reached hers April felt about as solid as air. His hands pressed her closer, and then her own hands drew his chest against her breasts.

His mouth was hot against hers, and confident.

If she'd been tentative, or if her brain had been capable of worrying about her kissing technique or other such nonsense, his assuredness would have erased it all.

But, as it was, April didn't feel at all unsure. In fact, Hugh made her feel that this kiss was about as right as anything could get.

His tongue brushed a question against her bottom lip and her own tongue was her crystal-clear answer. Her hands slid up his chest to entwine behind his neck and in his hair, tugging him even closer.

Their kiss was as intense as every moment between them, and as volatile. He kissed her hard, and soft, and voraciously. As if he could kiss her for ever, and as if they had all the time in the world.

But April was impatient.

She took the lead now, kissing him with everything she had and more. More than she'd thought she was capable of: with more passion, less control.

This was raw and passionate and…near desperate.

April wanted to be as close as she could be to him. She wanted him pressed up hard against her. She wanted to feel his solidity and his strength.

She wanted to feel his *skin*.

Her hands drifted down his back, skimming wide shoulder blades and the indentations of his spine. And then they slid beneath jacket and T-shirt to land at the small of his back. Against smooth, gorgeous, hot skin.

His hands followed a similar path, and his touch made her sigh into his mouth as it moved against her back, her stomach, and then upwards—against her ribs to the underside of her—

Something vibrated and Hugh went still.

He broke his lips away from hers, but not far. She could feel him breathe against her mouth as he spoke.

'My phone,' he said. 'I'm sorry.'

'Me too,' she said, all husky.

His smile was crooked. 'Yeah...'

Then he stepped away, and her skin felt bereft without his touch.

He fished his phone out of the back pocket of his jeans. It appeared to have been a notification vibration, not a call, and he turned slightly to scroll through his phone.

When he turned back to her, he just looked at her for long moments. At her still slightly askew jumper, at her lips that felt swollen, at her eyes that she knew were inviting him to pick up exactly where they'd just finished.

But he didn't.

Instead, he said, 'That probably shouldn't have happened.'

April blinked, her brain still foggy. 'Why?'

'Because you work for me. And your husband just left you.'

She shrugged. 'You definitely didn't take advantage of me,' she said. 'And the husband thing—that's my problem, not yours. Nothing about what just happened was a problem for me.'

Mila and Ivy's encouragement fuelled her. For all her misgivings up until their kiss, she didn't regret it one bit now. She felt amazing: alive, and strong, and sexy and feminine…

'I don't want a relationship with you, April.'

Ouch.

It shouldn't have hurt, but it did.

'And you thought the desperate divorcee must be keen to jump straight into another relationship?' Her tone was tart. She didn't give him time to respond. 'And also, that if I did, I'd want a relationship with *you*? That's rather presumptuous.'

April crossed her arms.

His forehead crinkled as he considered her words. 'I suppose it is,' he said. 'I apologise.'

April nodded sharply. 'Just to be clear—the *last* thing I want is a relationship. I was with my ex for a long time—I need to just be me for a while. That being said, I really liked what we just did. I'd like to do it again.'

She didn't know where this bravado came from.

She was practically propositioning Hugh Bennell. In fact, she definitely was. She was *propositioning* him.

Because that kiss… She'd never experienced anything like it. She'd never felt like this before and heat continued to traverse through her veins simply from the memory of his mouth against hers. His body against hers.

'I'd like to do it again, too,' he said. His gaze was steady and his words measured—as if he'd carefully considered her proposal before constructing his answer. 'But, I'd also like to be clear. I date, but that's it. I never take it further. I'm never anyone's boyfriend. I'll never be someone's husband. You need to be aware of that before this goes any further.'

April found herself fighting a smile in response to his seriousness. 'That seems a bit extreme,' she said. '*Never?* Really?'

'Really,' he said.

He didn't elaborate. He still looked at her with a determinedly serious expression.

'Well,' April said, smiling now, 'I must say my experience of marriage wasn't ultimately positive, so maybe you're onto something.'

His lips quirked now. 'It would seem so.'

'Okay,' she said. 'I can deal with that. No relationships. *Deal.*'

As she'd told Hugh, it was exactly the right thing for her. Quite honestly, the last thing she wanted was to leap from one relationship into another. But for some silly reason, Hugh's rejection of anything more with her still stung.

There was another noisy buzz as his phone, now on the kitchen bench, vibrated again.

'I need to go,' he said. 'I have a meeting. Can we do dinner? Tonight? I can email you the details.'

He was in business mode now, as efficient as his instructions and his emails.

'Sure,' she said. 'But I only have a few hours before my second job.'

He paused, looking up from his phone. 'How much extra would I need to pay you so you could quit that job?' he asked.

'Ah,' April said, 'that sounds like a conflict of interests. I don't think HR would approve of that.'

'I own the company,' Hugh pointed out. 'And I don't like rushing dinner.'

'Well, then, *I* don't approve,' April said firmly. 'Let's keep this professional.'

Hugh stepped closer—much closer. He leant down and spoke just millimetres from her lips. 'Sure,' he said, 'except for making out in the kitchen.'

Long minutes later they came up for air, and April lifted her fingers to her thoroughly kissed lips as Hugh finally walked away.

'Agreed,' she said, as the front door clicked shut.

* * *

The conference call was endless.

Hugh sat back in his chair, letting the wheels roll him back a small distance from his desk.

He'd docked his laptop, so the other attendees' faces were displayed on the large slender screen before him. Everybody else allowed their faces to be shown, so Hugh could see each of them: the red-headed product manager in Ireland, his gaze focused on his keyboard, the dark-haired user experience manager in Sydney, her attention focused on the slides that the senior developer, also in London, was showing them…

The developer was talking directly into his camera as he discussed some of the technical difficulties his team was currently encountering, his purple dreadlocks draped over his shoulders.

Of course, Hugh's face didn't appear.

Hugh still insisted upon that, despite the recommendations of the digital collaboration expert he'd engaged to improve the effectiveness of his widely dispersed team. Yes, he could see how a video feed might—as the consultant had advised—improve both rapport and communication, but no matter how large his company became he was still in charge. Hence—no cameras. For him, anyway.Even now, so many years later, old habits died hard. Because, of course, it wasn't about *him*. He didn't care if his colleagues saw him and his slightly too long hair and three-day-old beard.

It was about his *house*. Everyone on the conference call was in their home. This meeting had a backdrop of contrasting wallpapers and paint colours, of artwork and photographs, of bookcases and blinds and curtains.

Hugh wasn't going to contribute his home to that landscape. He didn't let anyone into his home. In any way. Ever.

Except April.

It seemed April had become the exception to several things.

Such as his structured approach to dating.

It had been timely that he'd received an alert from Ryan's dating app mid-kiss with April. It should've been a reminder that he already had a tried and true approach to meeting women. And that kissing an employee in his mother's kitchen was *not* his modus operandi.

Instead, he hadn't even bothered to open the profile of the woman he'd been so carefully matched to.

After all, he'd just experienced a kiss that made his pulse beat fast and his body tighten simply by the act of thinking about it. It had been all-consuming: a hot, intense phenomenon of a kiss. Which was, after all, the point. He dated. He liked women. He wanted to meet women who liked him. And he definitely wanted that spark of attraction. April ticked each and every one of those boxes. Except the spark was more like a bonfire.

So—why not?

If the parameters were made as clear to April Spencer as he always made sure they were with other women, what was the problem?

Logically, none.

Although somewhere right at the edge of his subconscious doubts did twinge.

But they were easily overcome. At the time he'd simply had to look at April to forget anything but his need to touch her again. Now he just needed to recall the shape of her waist and the heat of her skin beneath his palms.

When he did that there was no need to analyse it further.

CHAPTER NINE

APRIL HAD NEVER been more grateful for an unexpected delivery in her life. But she only had a minute to photograph her new peep-toe, sky-high ankle boots before heading out through the door.

Taking these lovelies out to dinner! #highheels #peeptoes #CovetMyShoesCo

She had hardly anything to wear, what with her nonexistent social life since arriving in London, but her new shoes teamed with black jeans and her dressiest shirt made her look marginally more glamorous than she did when unpacking cardboard boxes.

At least she'd recoloured her hair the week before, so there was no hint of her blonde roots. And she'd left her hair down, although there had been hardly any time for her to attempt some loose curls with her straightening iron. Back in Perth, she put more effort into getting ready to go to the supermarket.

Part of her was a little disappointed that she didn't have the time—or the money—to really go all out for Hugh. A lot disappointed, actually. But then—

did it matter? Hugh hadn't seem bothered by her dusty, messy-haired *dishabille* that morning.

Plus, it wasn't as if she needed to impress him. They'd both been pretty clear about what they wanted: each other. For a short time.

That was it. No complications. No relationship.

It should be…freeing.

But it wasn't. Instead this felt very much like a first date to her. A first date full of nerves and anticipation and possibilities.

April knew she couldn't think like that. It wasn't what Hugh was offering, and it wasn't what April wanted.

It wasn't.

She meant that with every cell in her body—except for that little chunk of her heart that had ached when Hugh had so summarily rejected her.

She supposed *I don't want a relationship with you, April* had too many echoes of Evan's *I don't love you* rejection not to hurt, at least just a little bit. She wouldn't be human if it didn't. Surely?

So it didn't mean anything.

She was strong and independent and single—and she had a date with Hugh Bennell.

April grabbed her scarf and coat, and headed for the Tube.

Hugh had booked the same table he always booked.

He figured that while April might not have been

matched with him by any computer algorithm, really tonight was no different from any other date.

Except for the fact she was his employee, and that he'd already kissed her...

No, he told himself firmly. There was nothing different or special *whatsoever* about tonight.

It was just a date.

And so they were at his favourite restaurant. A very nice restaurant, with white linen tablecloths and an epic wine list. Importantly, it valued the privacy of its customers, and kept tables well-spaced and the lighting intimate. He'd had many very pleasant dates here, with great food and robust conversation.

'This is lovely,' April said from across the table. She held a glass of sparkling water in her hand, and her long hair cascaded over one shoulder in chocolate waves. 'I wish I had more time to enjoy it properly. To be honest, I just thought we'd go to a pub.'

She started work at nine p.m., so they didn't even have two hours before she had to leave.

'I don't like pubs,' he said truthfully.

'Really? But London does them so well. There's a pub near your place I've been wanting to try for ages. But I'm such a Nigel now, I haven't had the opportunity.'

'Nigel?' Hugh asked.

'No Friends. You know? Nigel No Friends? Or is that another Australianism I didn't realise was one?'

Hugh grinned. 'Like Billy No Mates?' he prompted.

'Exactly,' April said, looking pleased. 'Seems being a loser is universal.'

He laughed out loud. 'I don't believe for a second that you don't have friends,' he said.

'Well, I *do* have friends,' April said. 'Just not here. And I've been working too much to meet anyone. Not that I particularly wanted to—especially at first. I just wanted to be on my mopey lonesome.'

'Not any more?'

'No,' she said firmly. 'I guess I'm a pretty social person usually. I'm always out—catching up with friends for coffee or lunch. Going to parties or—'

Her voice broke off, and he raised an eyebrow in question.

'Or…ah…the movies, or a bar, or whatever.'

Her gaze had slid downwards, was now focused on her bread and the untouched gold-wrapped pat of butter. She seemed suddenly uncomfortable.

But then she was refocusing on him, and the moment was gone as if it had never happened. 'So, once I get rid of this night-job nightmare, I'm hoping to finally get to explore London. So at the moment you're basically my only friend, as my housemates seem convinced I'm bordering on elderly at my advanced age—'

'I don't like pubs,' he repeated.

April blinked. 'Really?' she asked again, only

now seeming to realise that he hadn't elaborated on that. 'Why?'

He shrugged. 'I don't like people. And pubs are full of them.'

'No,' April said simply. 'Not true.'

'It *is* true,' Hugh said, with deliberate patience and the hint of a smile. 'They *are* full with *lots* of people.'

She shook her head. 'No, the bit about you not liking people. You like me.'

'You're not everyone,' he said.

His gaze slid over her as he reminded himself exactly how *not everyone* April Spencer was. She'd apologised when she'd arrived for her—as she'd described them—'casual clothes'. But personally Hugh thought she looked incredible, in skinny jeans that highlighted the curve of her hips and a colourfully abstract printed silk blouse that skimmed her breasts and revealed her lovely neck and collarbones. She'd painted her lips a classic red and her eyes were smoky and...

Narrowed.

Hugh sighed. 'Okay. I don't like people I don't know. Or hanging out with people I don't know in one, dark cramped place.'

'Okay,' she said. 'Then how do you meet people?'

'Women?' he clarified.

She might have blushed, but the lighting meant he couldn't be absolutely certain.

'Sure,' she said. 'Or men. Anyone. Just people.'

'Women—except you—I meet online. I prefer to set my expectations up-front, and there is no better way than in writing. And as for new mates—well, I've got friends from uni I'm still in touch with. That's enough. And I cycle with a group that lives locally, but that's not a social thing.'

'I *like* meeting new people,' April said, not surprising Hugh at all. 'Everyone has a story to tell, you know? Although I'm close to my sisters, so I've never really gone out of my way to find new *close* friends.'

She paused, looking thoughtful.

'I hadn't thought about dating yet—or online dating, I mean. When I met Evan we communicated with folded-up notes via our schoolfriends—not smartphones. But, yes, I can see the appeal of online. Seems very efficient for identifying deal-breakers. Although,' she said, leaning forward slightly, 'I've always kind of liked the idea of meeting someone random at a bar or in a pub. You know—the intrigue of it. Discovering little bits and pieces about them, revealing little bits about you, working out if you actually like each other or not. I never got to do that because I was with Evan since high school.'

'But it could be a total waste of everyone's time,'

Hugh said. 'The odds aren't high that you'll meet the person of your dreams one random night at a random pub.'

'Why not?' April said as their meals were served. April had ordered gnocchi, garnished with thin slices of parmesan. In front of Hugh was placed a steak. 'Don't you believe that some people are destined to meet?'

'No,' he said firmly. 'If you want to meet Mr Perfect and you find him at the pub, that's great. But it's just luck—not destiny. Online dating takes the luck out of it.'

April looked sceptical. 'I don't know about that. Perfect on paper is different to perfect in person. You can't guarantee chemistry.'

Hugh sliced off a small piece of steak, smothering it in mashed potato and mushroom sauce. 'In my experience the matching algorithm of the app I use does a pretty good job. And it also means that when there *is* chemistry it's with someone who wants the same things as you. There isn't much point having great chemistry if you both want completely different things.'

There was a long pause as they both ate, and April's concentration was aimed at her dinner plate.

'And you don't want a relationship ever? Why?' she asked.

He swallowed, barely tasting the delicious food. 'Isn't that a bit personal for a first date?'

April glanced up and looked determined. 'I told you that my husband left me because he didn't love me enough. We've been plenty personal.'

'"Enough"?'

She hadn't mentioned that word before, and he watched as she winced—but quickly hid it—when he repeated it.

She shrugged and put on a smile. 'Our love wasn't like in movies and books, apparently. I didn't elicit that level of emotion in him, it would seem. He met someone else who did.'

Her words were light, but he could see it still hurt her to say them.

'What a—' Hugh began, but then stopped. What was he going to say? *What a tosser?* For not loving April more?

He couldn't say that. After all, he was no better. He wasn't offering her anything: not a relationship, and certainly not love.

If her ex-husband was an idiot, what was *he*?

A realist. Not someone caught up in imaginary stories and Hollywood fairytales.

But he knew he didn't want to hurt April. So she deserved the truth.

'I'm happier on my own,' he said. 'I don't feel any urge to share my life with anyone.'

'But you date?' she prompted. 'You just said that you meet women online.'

He nodded and reached for his bourbon. 'That has absolutely nothing to do with sharing my life.'

'Ah,' April said. 'So it's just about the sex.'

Hugh coughed on his drink. But her directness made him smile. 'Well, I also just *like* women, and spending time in the company of women.'

'Just not in pubs, and you never share any of your life with them?'

'Yes,' he said. 'That pretty much sums it up.'

April tilted her head, studying him carefully. Her gaze drifted across his hair, his nose, his lips, then downwards across his off-white open-necked shirt, along the shape of his arms to his wrist and his heavy, stainless steel watch.

She met his gaze again. 'You're weird,' she said.

Hugh laughed. 'I've been told that before.' He shrugged now. 'But it's who I am. Take it or leave it.'

He'd said that casually, with no real intent. But he could see April turning it over in her mind. Really *he* should be turning it over in *his* mind. She was clearly emotionally vulnerable, for all her brave words.

He believed her when she said she wasn't ready for a relationship. But she definitely wasn't ready to be hurt again.

And he'd hurt women before, despite all his sign-posting and expectation-setting. With those women he'd reconciled the situation with an almost 'buyer beware' lack of emotion. Although of course he hadn't *liked* it that he'd caused anyone pain. In his quest to avoid the complications of relationships the last thing he wanted was to cause the kind of despair he'd observed in his mother's many failed relationships.

But with April—he'd kissed her before telling her any of this. He'd invited her out for dinner before she'd had a chance to catch her breath after that crazy hot kiss in the kitchen.

She'd be smart to walk away. *He* should walk away. This was already far more complicated than any other date he'd been on.

But he didn't.

And she didn't.

'Tell me about your company,' she said, 'What's actually involved in creating a new app? I've always wondered...'

And so they changed the subject, and the conversation became as pleasant and robust as on every other date he'd had at this restaurant.

For a short while.

Then it became easy and rambling, as April told him about a camping trip to northern Western Australia with her sisters as a child, and he told her about how he'd discovered cycling a few years ago and now had seen more of the UK on his bike than he'd ever thought possible. They talked about nothing serious—certainly nothing as serious as divorce or relationships.

As their desserts arrived, and April started to tell him about an amazing frozen dessert she'd had once in a food court in Singapore, she realised the time.

'Oh, crap—I'm late,' she said urgently.

And then she was up, her bag slung over her shoulder and her coat over her arm, leaving her half-eaten dessert. She was a few steps away from the table before he knew what was happening.

A moment later his hand was on her elbow, slowing her.

Then he kissed her.

It was supposed to be quick—he knew she was late. But it wasn't.

They both lingered. It wasn't a passionate kiss—they were standing in the middle of a restaurant and he hadn't forgotten that. But his lips tasted hers for long moments, and then their gazes tangled wordlessly after their mouths had parted.

'I need to go,' she whispered.

So Hugh returned to his table to eat his parfait alone.

* * *

The next day was Saturday.

April had slept in, and the late-rising December sun had already been in the sky for at least an hour.

Her roommate lay curled up in a multi-coloured duvet bundle on her bed, her slow, deep breathing indicating she was still sound asleep.

Quietly April retrieved her phone from where it was charging, and propped herself up in bed to scroll through her Instagram and Facebook feeds.

The ankle boots had been a hit, and she had hundreds of 'likes' and comments. She replied to a few before opening up her instant messenging account, which had a little red circle on it indicating she'd missed a heap of messages.

All from her sisters.

They'd caught up for lunch in Perth while she'd been sleeping, and had sent a photo of them both—and baby Nate—sitting cross-legged on a patchwork quilt at King's Park, towering trees and a playground in the background.

Mila: Wish you were here!

Neither of her sisters was currently online, but April typed a reply anyway:

April: I miss you all so much!

Her roommate rolled over in bed. April had nothing against Fiona personally, but she *hated* not having her own space.

She started a new message.

April: I have so much to tell you. Something happened with Mr Mysterious...

But then she stopped and deleted everything she'd just written.

It felt...too soon.

For what?

She put her phone down and headed for the bathroom before the rest of her late-rising housemates woke up.

Under the sting of hot water she closed her eyes, remembering that kiss in the restaurant.

She'd spent a lot of time remembering it as she'd unloaded pallets at the supermarket and stacked shelves until one a.m.

For some reason it was that last kiss that she kept replaying. It hadn't been as sexy as their first kiss but it had been... Unexpected. And differently unexpected from that first remarkable unexpected kiss in the kitchen.

Because she knew how intensely private Hugh was. Yet he'd kissed her in a room full of strangers.

What did it mean?

Nothing.

She squeezed face-wash onto her palm and scrubbed her face much harder than necessary.

No. He'd explained that when he dated he was clear about what he wanted. That was all it was.

A few minutes later, with a towel wrapped around her, she made a phone call. After all, she could be clear about what she wanted, too.

'Hugh Bennell,' he answered, in his amazing low and sexy voice.

'I know that I was only supposed to use this number in an emergency,' April said, remembering his instructions on the day they'd met. 'But this *is* an emergency.'

'What's wrong?' he asked, sharply.

'I need someone to have all-day breakfast with me at the best all-day breakfast place in London.'

She could sense his smile. 'And where is that?'

'I don't know,' she said. 'I'll look it up and let you know where to meet me?'

'Done,' he said. 'See you soon.'

April was smiling as she typed *Best all-day breakfast London* into her phone.

Based on reviews, and reasonable proximity to where they both lived, April had chosen a simple corner café in Clerkenwell that had red gingham curtains on the windows and white-tiled walls inside covered with black-framed old newspaper articles.

She ordered coffee while she was waiting for Hugh, and spent way too much time trying to select a table—*where to sit if your date doesn't like random people?*—before just grabbing a table by the window. She still felt very much like a tourist, and welcomed the opportunity to overlook a classic London streetscape. Hugh could always suggest they move if he wasn't comfortable.

While she waited she scrolled through the remaining photos from her shoot back in Perth, trying to work out which to use next. She only had five more left, so if she really stretched it out maybe five weeks before she needed to sort out what she was doing.

Or at the very least reveal her new hair colour.

Although even now she was losing followers—and definitely losing engagement. Her research had shown that optimum post frequency for follower growth was, on average, around one point five posts a day. Since her move to London she was down to about a post every two days. And, as she was rationing the shoot photos, very few had her physically *in* them—or at least all of her—and she knew that photos of her coffee, or her feet, or her fingernails, or the book she was reading, or shots of the sunset—*thanks, Carly*—were never going to be highperforming posts.

It wasn't great. Not for her 'April Molyneux brand'—for want of a better phrase—and certainly not for the foundation. Her follower numbers were critical when it came to enticing brands to work with her. She couldn't afford for those numbers to continue to drop.

'Blonde?'

It was Hugh—behind her. Absorbed in her phone, and her thoughts, April hadn't heard him approach.

'Oh!' she said, automatically pushing the button to make her phone screen black. 'Hi! Is this table okay? I know there are people around, but it's such a nice view...'

She was talking fast, mentally kicking herself for letting him see the photos.

'It's fine,' he said, pulling out a chair. 'It's just crowded places that I don't like. This is fine.' He gestured towards her phone. 'Can I have a look? I can't imagine you blonde.'

April couldn't think of any plausible reason not to show Hugh. Reluctantly, she handed the phone to him. 'It was just a silly photo shoot that a friend did with me. It was supposed to make me feel better after Evan.'

That excuse worked, as the photos had been taken in different outfits, and all over Perth.

Hugh nodded as he flicked through the images, and April prayed that she wouldn't receive a message or an email or notification—because if he inadvertently opened up an app her real name would be plastered all over her social media accounts.

But thankfully he simply handed her phone back after what was probably less than a minute.

'Blonde is nice,' he said, 'but I like you brunette.'

So did April. Colouring her hair had been more symbolic than a fashion statement, but she was so glad she'd done it. Her natural hair colour was a pale brownish blonde, but she'd been highlighting it for years. The dark chocolate colour she had now was flattering—and strikingly different. But then, wasn't *she*? Sitting here, in this café, watching London pass by, she didn't feel anything like the woman she'd been before Evan left her.

'Thank you,' she said, and slid a menu across the table towards him.

She already knew what she was going to order, and she needed a moment to think.

She'd just lied to Hugh. A white lie, possibly—because, technically, it *had* been a photo shoot. Just not only for herself. But for her million followers.

Did it matter?

Last night at dinner, despite a few near misses, it hadn't been too difficult to avoid revealing who she was. Because, really, her family's fortune wasn't relevant first date conversation.

And it wasn't as if she was hiding the important stuff: he knew she was getting divorced, he knew a

bit about her family—skimming over the details—
and now he knew she'd happily eat breakfast for
every meal.

And—really—did she owe him any more than
that? In this relationshipless, life-sharing no-go
zone, did her billion-dollar trust fund, million social media followers and socialite lifestyle make any
difference? Especially when he thought she was a
penniless backpacker?

Yes, said her gut.

No, reasoned her brain.

'I know what I want,' Hugh said, nodding at his
menu.

In the midday sun that streamed through the
window he squinted a little. He even did that at-
tractively, somehow. And with his stubble-less jaw—
he'd clearly shaved—he looked so darkly handsome
that April's heart skipped a beat.

'Do you?' he asked.

'Mmm...' she said. Then blinked, and swallowed.
'Yes,' she said more firmly. 'I do.'

He went to stand, but April put her hand on his
arm. 'No,' she said. 'I'll order. This is my treat.'

So she went to the counter to order breakfast that
she really couldn't afford, waiting in line behind a
couple. They were older than April, and looked bliss-
fully happy: the man's hand was wrapped loosely

around the woman's waist, his thumb hooked into her belt loop.

April glanced back at their table and went still when she realised Hugh was watching her. His gaze was intense. And appreciative. It made her feel hot and liquid inside.

A sharp but low-pitched word drew April's attention. The happy couple were arguing about something in harsh staccato whispers that continued as they walked back to their table.

Now, *that* looked complicated.

Relationships *were* complicated.

So why complicate things by revealing the truth?

She ordered their breakfast and walked back to Hugh, table number in her hand.

He smiled at her, and she smiled back.

Yes. She definitely knew what she wanted.

Hugh.

Without complications.

CHAPTER TEN

AFTER LUNCH HUGH played tour guide as he and April spent the afternoon walking through London. They chatted as they ambled the mile from Clerkenwell to St Paul's Cathedral, then headed across the Millennium Bridge and along the Thames. Beside the river they stopped occasionally to lean against the stone and iron barrier and watch the boats float by, for April to take photos of the sparkling silver skyscraper skyline beyond Canary Wharf, or for April to ask questions about the height of The Shard or how often Tower Bridge opened to allow ships through.

This wasn't his usual Saturday.

He'd gone for his early-morning group cycle ride as normal, and had been reading the newspaper at his dining table when April had called.

Usually he'd spend the rest of his Saturday maybe lifting weights in his spare room, or binge-watching something that looked interesting. Later, he'd work. He always did at the weekend.

So, nothing critical.

But still… After he'd agreed to meet April so readily he'd felt uneasy. Maybe because it hadn't even occurred to him to say no.

He'd told April he liked spending time with women, which of course he did. But at dinner. At night. On a date.

Not casually. Not wearing jeans and trainers and without an actual plan.

So he'd decided he'd just have breakfast with April, then go home. That would be okay—no different from the night before.

Instead here he was. Willingly being her tour guide after she'd asked him so sweetly—with a big smile and those gorgeous eyes. And he was in no hurry to get home.

In fact he was having fun.

And having fun with April was so easy. He only felt uneasy when he reminded himself that he should be. Which was crazy, right? April had said he was weird, and he knew he was. But he wasn't a masochist.

He was having fun, and he and April were on exactly the same page. He needed to get over it—and himself—and just go with the flow.

He reached out, grabbing her fingers as she walked beside him. He tugged at her hand, pulling her to the side of the footpath and then pulling her towards him.

Hugh kissed her thoroughly, his hands at her back and her waist and hers tangled in his hair.

'Wow,' she said when they came up for air.

He murmured against her ear. 'I realised I hadn't kissed you today,' he said.

That he'd waited so long seemed impossible.

He felt her smile as he kissed her jaw. 'Where did you learn to kiss like that?' she asked on a sigh.

'Rachael Potter in the Upper Sixth asked if she could practise on me,' Hugh said, grinning against the skin of her cheek. 'She was a year older than me—an older woman. At the time it was the most thrilling moment of my life. Although I wasn't to tell a soul, of course.'

April stepped back, still meeting his gaze. 'Why not?'

'Because—as we determined last night—I'm weird. As an adult, I'm fortunate that people just consider me a little idiosyncratic. In high school I was just plain strange.'

'But why would people think that?'

Hugh shrugged and started walking again, his hands stuffed into his coat pockets.

'It's like I told you—I didn't want anyone to know about the house. As a young kid it was just easier to not have any friends. It wasn't until uni—you know, when playdates aren't really expected—that I had friends again.'

'That's sad,' April said. 'I'm sure most kids wouldn't have cared.'

Hugh raised his eyebrows. 'I was already the nerdy computer kid. I wasn't about to sign up as the kid with the crazy mother. And I definitely wasn't going to let my mum be thought of like that.'

They kept on walking. Around them it was dusk, and the trees that lined the Thames were beginning to twinkle with hundreds of blue lights that grew brighter as the sun retreated.

'Not that it made any difference,' Hugh said, minutes later. 'Kids still whispered about my mum. And about me. Maybe some kids would've been fine with it, but I didn't let anyone close enough to find out. I was moody—and resentful that I had to look after my mum.'

'Look after her?' April asked.

They were still walking, and Hugh kept his gaze on the concrete footpath.

'Yeah,' he said. 'Eventually it was more than just *stuff* that Mum was collecting. There were piles of rubbish. Piles of dirty laundry. I had to create a safe passage for her to get to bed each night. I had to make sure her bed was clear of crap and her sheets were clean. I did all the shopping...the cooking. I remembered to do my homework. I packed my own lunches.'

'She wasn't well,' April said.

'No,' Hugh said with a humourless laugh. 'And I was too young to really understand that. I'd researched hoarding at the library, and I'd tried to help—but even though I kind of got that it must be some sort of anxiety disorder, I wasn't really sympathetic. All I saw was that she managed to go to work each day. She managed to socialise, to continue her quest to find the perfect man, and yet we lived in this absolute horror story of a house that *I* had to keep liveable even as she brought more and more crap inside it.'

April remained silent, letting him speak.

He stopped again. They stood beneath a cast-iron lamppost with dolphins twined around its base—one of many that lit the South Bank.

'So, yeah…' Hugh said. 'Rachael Potter didn't want anyone to know she was kissing the weird, friendless geek with the crazy mother.'

April reached out and held his hand. 'What happened to her?' she asked. 'To your mum?'

He'd known this question was coming.

He swallowed, angry that his throat was tight and that his heart ached and felt heavy.

'Cancer,' he said. 'I always thought her hoarding would kill her, but I was wrong. It was unexpected—quick and brutal—and she told me in the hospital that she wanted to come home to die. I thought that was bizarre—that she would want to be in the house that represented all she'd lost when Len had died, illustrated with box after box. But she did, so I organised to have her room cleared, to make it safe for a hospital bed to be delivered.'

He swallowed, staring at their joined hands.

'But it was already too late. Before the first box was moved she died.'

Suddenly April's arms were around him.

She was hugging him, her arms looped around his neck, her cheek pressed against his shoulder. She hugged him as he stood there, stiff and wooden, his hands firm by his sides.

She hugged him for long minutes until—eventually—he hugged her back. Tight and hard, with her body pressed tight against him.

He wasn't a hugger—he'd told her that. Even if he was, he'd had no one to hug when his mother had died. At the time it hadn't mattered. It hadn't even occurred to him that he might need or want someone to hug, to grieve with.

As always, it had just been him.

Eventually they broke apart. He turned from April, wiping at the tears that had threatened, but thankfully hadn't been shed.

When he caught April's gaze again, her own gaze travelled across his face in the lamplight, but she said nothing.

He didn't want to be standing here any longer.

'Want a drink?' he asked.

April blinked, but nodded. 'Let's go.'

They headed up a series of narrow cobblestoned lanes, Hugh still holding April's hand. His strides were long, and April had to hurry to keep pace with him.

He hadn't said a word, and April wasn't really sure what to say.

Then he stopped in front of a small bar. Beyond black-framed windows April could see exposed brick walls and vintage velvet couches.

'Want to try here?' Hugh asked.

She was confused. 'You don't like bars.'

He grinned. 'I don't like *people*. It's still early—hardly anyone's here.'

She followed Hugh inside. The bar's warmth was a welcome relief. It wasn't entirely empty, but only two other customers were there: two women in deep conversation, cocktails in hand.

At the bar, April ordered red wine and Hugh bourbon. April chose one of the smaller couches, towards the rear of the rectangular space, and ran her fingers aimlessly over the faded gold fabric as Hugh sat down. With Hugh seated the couch seemed significantly smaller—their knees bumped, in fact, his dark blue denim against her faded grey.

Not that April minded.

'So,' Hugh said, 'tell me about *your* first kiss.'

His tone was light, and the pain she'd glimpsed in his eyes beneath the lamppost had disappeared.

'Well,' she said, 'I was six. Rory Crothers. Kiss-chasey.' She sighed expansively. 'It was *amazing*!'

Hugh's lips quirked. 'Doesn't count,' he said.

She widened her eyes. 'You mean Rachael Potter *didn't* just give you a kiss on the cheek?'

'No,' he said. Straight-faced.

'Ah…' April said. 'So we're talking *tongue* kissing, then?'

Hugh gave a burst of laughter. 'Yeah,' he said. 'Definitely tongue kissing.'

The look in his eyes was smouldering—and April knew it had *nothing* to do with young Miss Potter.

Something suddenly occurred to her, and she leant forward, resting her hand on Hugh's thigh. 'Am I flirting with a guy in a pub?' she asked.

He grinned, obviously remembering their conversation from the night before. 'Just like you always wanted.'

She smiled. 'This is just as fun as I'd imagined.'

Hugh's eyes flicked downwards to her hand on his thigh. 'Yep,' he said.

Someone had turned up the music, and the beat reverberated around them. As they'd been talking a handful of customers had walked in, were now standing in a group only a few metres away from them.

She nodded in their direction. 'Still okay?' she asked.

He nodded.

'Well,' April said, returning to his original question, 'this is going to sound really sad, but if we're only counting tongue kissing, then Evan was it. I was sixteen, and he kissed me on my front doorstep when I was his date for his high school ball.'

'So I'm only the second guy you've kissed?'

She nodded.

He took a long drink of his bourbon. 'I know you said you met in high school, but I hadn't really considered what that actually meant.'

April tilted her head quizzically. 'It means I met him in high school.'

'You were with him half your life. You grew from teenager to adult with him. That's a really big deal.'

'None of this is news to me,' she said dryly, then sipped her wine.

'And he left *you*?'

April blinked. 'What is this? Remind-April-Of-Crap-Stuff-That's-Happened Day?'

She sounded hurt and defensive, which she didn't like.

Hugh was silent, and she knew she didn't have to answer his question if she didn't want to. He'd be okay about it. But for some reason she started talking.

'He left me,' she began, 'and I've been telling people I didn't see it coming, but that's a lie.'

April paused, this time taking a long drink of her wine.

'We were having problems for years—even before we got married. It's probably why we took more than ten years to get married, actually. But it was nothing serious—just issues with communicating. Different expectations about stuff—when we'd have kids…that type of thing. So we went to counselling and we tried talking about it. I guess for me, after such a long time, ending it just didn't feel like an option. Evan had been part of my entire adult life, and I couldn't imagine life without him. So I didn't. But obviously Evan had no issues with imagining his life without *me*.'

April watched her fingers as she drew lines in the velvet of the couch.

'I was really keen to have a baby, and we started trying pretty much as soon as we got married—three years ago. But that was all my idea. Evan just went along with it. Maybe that's when he started wondering if things could be different—I don't know.'

Her hair had fallen forward and she tucked the long strands behind her ears as she looked back up at Hugh. Over his shoulder, she saw that more people had entered the bar, and now more couches were occupied than empty.

'I thought he was the love of my life right until the end. I mean, relationships are *supposed* to be hard at times, so I didn't see any red flags when we were having problems. I probably should have. But, yeah, Evan was right. We didn't have that epic, all-consuming love that you see in movies.' She looked at her glass, swirling the deep red liquid but not drinking. 'Although,' she said, 'I think now I realise that I always loved him more than he loved me.'

That last bit had come from nowhere, and April went still as she realised the truth of what she'd said. A truth she hadn't allowed herself to acknowledge before.

'Do you still love him?'

Her gaze flew from her glass to meet Hugh's. He was looking at her with...*concern*? With *pity*?

She sat up, removing her hand from his leg.

'Why?' she asked. 'Would you prefer it that I still do?'

'That wasn't why I was asking,' he said.

April didn't understand why she'd reacted this way, but anger out of nowhere shot through her veins. 'If I still loved him you wouldn't have to worry about the poor, rejected divorcee getting too attached to you, would you? That would keep things neater.'

'April—' he began.

But she wasn't ready to listen. The still raw pain of Evan's rejection was colliding with Hugh's pity.

Pity from yet another man who didn't want a relationship with her.

'Why do you care, anyway? What do you know about love, Mr Never-Had-A-Relationship?'

'I care,' he said.

But that was just too much.

She put her glass down on a low table, then stood up and headed for the door.

After a few steps she realised just how crowded the bar had become. There was no clear path for her to take.

She turned back to Hugh, who—as she'd known he would—had followed her. He was only a step behind her. As she watched, a heavy-set bloke turned and accidentally banged his beer against Hugh's arm, spilling the liquid down Hugh's jacket. The man apologised profusely, and a moment later April was at Hugh's side as he reassured the other man and waved him away.

April was standing right in front of Hugh now. They were surrounded—a big group must have entered the bar together—and suddenly the space had gone from busy to absolutely packed. The air was heavy with the smell of aftershave and beer.

Hugh's jaw was tense beneath the bar's muted lighting.

'Are you okay?' she asked.

Hugh's expression was dismissive. 'I'll get it dry-cleaned. It was just an accident.'

'No, not that,' she said. 'I mean—you know—all the people?'

'It doesn't matter. Why did you walk away?'

Someone tapped on April's shoulder and asked to squeeze past, which moved April closer to Hugh.

She lifted her chin. 'I don't want you feeling sorry for me,' she said. 'I'm fine. I don't need your pity.'

'I don't *pity* you, April,' he said, low and harsh in her ear. 'But you've been hurt badly. This might not be a good idea.'

He meant *them*.

'You want to end it?'

'No.' He said it roughly. Firmly. His gaze told her he still felt every bit of the sizzling connection be-tween them. 'But I should.'

'Ah...' April said, nodding slowly. 'You're being *noble*.'

'Well—'

She cut him off. 'Thanks, but no thanks. I didn't sign up for you to be my knight in shining armour, Hugh. I get to make my own decisions. And, if nec-essary, my own mistakes.'

'You also didn't sign up for my relationship quirks.'

'You mean all your relationship rules and expec-tations? I get that you don't like it that I haven't fol-lowed your rules, but you've been crystal-clear. No relationship. I get it, Hugh, and I'm going to be okay. I'm not fragile. You're not going to break me.'

Or her heart.

She wouldn't allow it.

Another clumsy patron bumped into April's back, pushing her into Hugh's chest. Her forearms landed flush against him, her hands splayed across his shoulders.

According to Hugh, she had a choice here: one was to push her arms against him and walk away. But that wasn't an option for April.

She'd spent months in a fog, questioning so much about her life and all that she'd once taken for granted. Everything was different for her now: her present *and* her future. Her life would not unfold the way she'd always expected it to.

But she didn't question this.

She knew now why she'd reacted so strongly to Hugh's concern, and to what she'd perceived as his pity. She *never* wanted someone to be with her unless she was the person they most *wanted* to be with. Her marriage hadn't been perfect, but she'd still not wanted anyone but Evan. And Evan had aspired to something more.

God, that *hurt.*

So she didn't want Hugh to feel sorry for her. She wanted him to *want* her.

And he did.

Right now he wanted to be with no one more than her. She believed that with every cell of her body: with every cell in her body that was now hot and liquid, thanks to the way his chest, belly and legs were pressed so close against hers. So what if he only wanted her *right now* and not for longer?

It didn't matter—because she *knew* that right at this moment she didn't need to worry about not being 'enough', or to worry if the man she was with was wondering if there was something—someone— *more* out there for him.

Right now Hugh wanted *her*. Just her. No one else.

It might not be about love or relationships or a future together, but it still felt good. Great. The best, even. It still felt like exactly what she needed. And, yeah, she definitely wanted Hugh more than anyone. She could barely think with him this close to her.

Her hands relaxed and shifted, one moving up to his hair. Her body softened against him. She loved how hard and solid every inch of him was. His hands, which had been at his sides, now moved. They slid across her hips to her back.

April stood on tiptoes to murmur against his lips. 'You know, there's something else I've always wanted to do in a pub,' she said. 'Kiss a hot—'

He silenced her with his mouth, kissing her thoroughly—with lips *and* tongue.

Yes, this was a *proper* kiss: sexy and playful, deep and soft and hard.

When her eyes slid shut April forgot about where they stood, forgot about the crowd, and she couldn't hear the music or the blur of conversation around them. It was just her and Hugh—the hot stranger she'd always wanted to kiss in a bar.

Although after today he didn't feel like a stranger. They'd had some big conversations. They'd shared each other's pain. Surely *that* didn't follow Hugh's rules...

But beneath Hugh's mouth, his teeth, his tongue, her ability for coherent analysis no longer existed. Instead she just got to feel—the strength of his shoulders, the heat of his mouth. And to react as she took her turn to lead their kiss, to explore his mouth and to lose herself in delicious sensation.

And then, just as Hugh's hand slid beneath her shirt and jacket, the heat of his touch shocking against the cool skin of her waist, yet another person bumped into them.

Hugh dragged his mouth from hers to speak into her ear. 'Can we get out of here?'

'Please,' she said.

And, holding Hugh's hand, April navigated them through the sea of bodies and noisy conversations finally to spill out onto the cobblestones outside.

Hugh tugged her a few metres away from the

doorway into the shadows of a neighbouring shop-front, the shop now closed in the evening darkness.

'Still hate pubs?' April asked, breathless as he backed her up against the wooden door.

'Intensely,' he said, his breath hot against her skin. 'But I really like this.'

And then he kissed her again.

CHAPTER ELEVEN

'DO YOU THINK it's a form of claustrophobia?' April asked as they were driven through London in the back seat of a black cab.

'The pub thing?' Hugh said, relaxing into his seat.

Streetlights intermittently lit the car's interior as they drove, painting April in light and shadow.

'No,' he continued. 'If anything it would be ochlophobia, which is a fear of crowds. But "fear" is too strong a word. Intolerance of crowds is more accurate.'

He'd researched his dislike of bustling, enclosed spaces, much as he'd researched his mother's hoarding. It hadn't been much of a leap to realise that if his mother had an anxiety-related disorder then possibly he did too.

But the label wasn't a comfortable fit. And certainly his issues were nowhere near as extreme as his mother's.

Tonight, for instance.

He *never* would've walked into that bar if it had been busy when they'd arrived. And, truthfully, while he'd been aware of the small space filling and people growing rowdier, the longer he and April had talked, the less it had bothered him.

His focus has been on April. Solely on April.

Later, as the crowds had buffeted them both, the familiar cloak of tension had wrapped around him. He had definitely wanted out of that bar, as rapidly as possible. But then April had asked if he was okay. And then it had become about *her* again—about his clearly unwanted concern for her—and then, soon after, about his need to touch her.

When he'd kissed her he wouldn't have cared if he'd been surrounded by a million people—he wouldn't have noticed. He'd been entirely and completely focused on April and on kissing her.

Surely if he truly had a phobia he wouldn't have been able to just forget about it like that? Just for a kiss?

In the rare times he'd found himself in a crowded space in the past fifteen years he certainly wouldn't have expected a kiss to have distracted him from the way his throat would tighten and his heart would race. But a kiss *had*.

Or maybe it was April?

He didn't let himself spend any time considering that.

'It isn't even crowds in general,' Hugh said, talking to silence his brain. 'I can go to the movies, to the theatre, without much problem. I generally go outside during intermissions, and I never wait around in the foyer before a show, but once I'm in my seat I'm fine, because it's an ordered, organised crowd. Also, I generally have a date if I'm going somewhere like that, so I'm not expected to converse with random people. Something else I don't enjoy. That's why the café today was fine—there wasn't a mass of people and I was there with you.'

'So you need white space?' April said.

He hadn't thought of it quite like that before, but the analogy worked.

'Like in your flat,' she said. 'That's like one big ocean of white space.'

His lips quirked. 'Yes,' he said. 'I suppose it is.'

The antithesis of the home he grew up in.

The cab slowed to a stop outside an uninspiring town house with a collection of dead weeds in a planter box at the front window. They'd arrived at April's place—a destination they'd chosen after having had a group of passing teenagers wolf-whistle as they'd been mid-kiss within that shop doorway and April had whispered, 'I should go home.'

He still felt the stab of disappointment at those words. But she was right to slow things down—even if it was the last thing he wanted to do.

He asked the cab driver to wait as he escorted April to the door. A sensor light flicked on and then almost immediately fizzled out, leaving April to search around in her handbag for keys in almost pitch-darkness.

'I hate this house,' April said when she eventually slid the key into the lock. 'Like, with a deep and abiding passionate hatred, you know?'

'So you're not going to invite me in?' he asked with a smile.

'No,' April said. 'Because I am certain two-day-old pizza remains on the coffee table and the fridge stinks like something died in it. And because I have a roommate—literally. And also because I'm trying to be sensible.'

But it seemed whenever Hugh was this close to April, being sensible just didn't feel like an option. So he kissed her again.

She kissed him back in a way that confirmed what he already knew—that April didn't want to be particularly sensible either.

'Do you want to—?' he began.

Come back to my place.

What was he *doing*?

'Do I want to what?' April asked. Her words were a husky whisper.

'Nothing,' he said firmly, stepping away. 'Nothing.'

He *never* invited a woman back to his place. It was, as April had so accurately said, his white space. Unadulterated with clutter or complications. *Any* complications.

He was halfway back to the cab before he'd even realised he was retreating.

'Hugh?'

'Bye, April,' he said, knowing he should say more, but unable to work out what.

He didn't give her a chance to respond and slid into the back seat of the cab, then watched her step into the townhouse, turn on the light and close the front door behind her.

Hugh knew he'd just reacted poorly. That he was being weird. But then, that was what he did. It was who he was.

He didn't have unexpected, amorphous day-long dates with women who worked for him. All of today had been exceedingly weird for him. It just hadn't felt weird at the time. At all, really—even now.

Being with April had felt natural. Inviting her to his place—*almost*—had felt natural, too.

But as the cab whisked him home he felt more comfortable with his decision with every passing mile. He'd been right to halt his rebellious tongue and his rebellious libido.

This thing with April was definitely breaking *some* of his rules. But not the important ones: No sleepovers at his house. No relationships.

Those rules were non-negotiable.

And those rules would never be broken.

* * *

April: I have some news.

Mila: Yes?

Ivy wasn't online, but April messaged both her sisters so Ivy could comment later if she wanted. She needed their advice.

It was Sunday morning, her roommate was once again sleeping in and this wasn't a conversation she wanted to have in the kitchen, with her other house-mates listening in. So instant messaging it was.

She snuggled under her doona and typed out a brief summary of the past forty-eight hours. It seemed completely impossible that it had been less than two days since Hugh had kissed her—it felt like for ever ago.

She closed her eyes as the memory of his lips at the sensitive skin beneath her ear made her shiver.

April: So what do you think?

She'd just described the way Hugh had practically run from her front doorstep after she'd been certain he intended to invite her back to his place.

Mila: I think he was just following your lead. You slowed things down, so he did too.

Mila's interpretation seemed logical, but April wasn't so sure.

April: I didn't want to slow things down. But it seemed the right thing to do.

Honestly, until those teenagers had whistled at them, slowing things down had been the absolute last thing on her mind.

Mila: Why?

April: Because I don't know anything about dating. Isn't there some protocol about what number date you sleep with someone on?

Ivy: No.

April grinned as her sister announced her appearance. Ivy's now husband had started as a one-night stand.

Ivy: But seriously. Do whatever feels right for you. This guy has made it clear that he doesn't want commitment, so you don't owe him anything. Do what you want, when you want. Date numbers are meaningless.

April: But the way he just left made me feel like he was having second thoughts.

Mila: Maybe he is.

April: Ouch!

Mila: Just ask him if you're not sure. What do you have to lose?

April: My job, I guess.

But she didn't really think so. Hugh wouldn't fire her—he'd just make sure their paths didn't cross.

Ivy posted a serious of furious emoticons.

April grinned.

April: No, don't worry. I'm one hundred per cent sure he wouldn't fire me.

Ivy: Good. I didn't think your taste in men was that bad.

April: It's not bad, just limited.

To two guys—one she'd married. She felt utterly clueless.

Mila: Exactly! So just ask him if he wants to help you expand your experience or not. Then you'll know.

Ivy: Good euphemism. And good plan. You don't want to waste time on a guy who isn't interested.

Ivy was right. On her bad days, April already felt she'd wasted almost half her life with Evan.

April: But what if he says no?

She paused before she sent the message.

She already knew what her sisters would say: they'd reassure that he wouldn't, or tell her that if he did it was his loss, not hers, or that if he did he was an idiot...blah-blah-blah.

Which would be lovely of them, but it wouldn't make a difference, would it?

Of course not.

If Hugh rejected her, then it was going to hurt. There was no sugar-coating that.

She deleted the words, thanked her sisters for their advice and then they chatted awhile longer.

Later, she responded to some comments on the latest post to her Instagram account—one of those blonde images from months ago.

For the first time she felt a little uncomfortable doing so. Until now her double life hadn't been impacting anyone: her family and those close to her knew exactly where she was and what she was doing. She'd felt a little guilty hiding such a big move from her followers, but she'd justified it with her confidence that they would understand when she eventually made her grand reveal. As for her suppliers and sponsors—well, she was ensuring that she was showcasing their products just as she would if she was living her life as April Molyneux, so there was no issue there.

So it was just Hugh that was making her feel this way.

You don't owe him anything.

Mila's remembered words helped April dismiss her concerns. She was over-complicating a situation that was supposed to be uncomplicated. Nothing had changed since she'd made her decision at the breakfast café.

There was no need to tell him.

On Monday, April decided to be very civilised—and, she imagined, very British—by inviting Hugh for a cup of tea. She sent him a text message practically the moment she arrived at the house:

April: Cup of tea? I'm just boiling the kettle.

Hugh's response was to simply walk in the front door a couple of minutes later.

'Good morning,' he said.

'Morning,' said April. She'd made—she hoped—a subtle effort in her appearance. She was still dressed for work, in jeans, a button-down shirt and sneakers, but she'd made a more concerted effort with her hair and make-up. Her ponytail was sleek, her make-up natural but polished.

Her intent had been to give herself a boost of confidence.

In reality it made everything feel like a very big deal. After a whole Sunday convincing herself it was anything but.

'I'm sorry about how I left,' Hugh said from across the marble countertop.

April nodded, then held out a small box full of teabags she'd found in one of the cupboards, so Hugh could select the type he wanted. April was more of a coffee girl, and she dumped a generous teaspoon of coffee granules into her Dockers mug as she waited for Hugh to elaborate.

'I panicked, I think,' he said.

April's gaze leapt to his. She didn't think that Hugh was a man who often admitted to panic—of any kind.

'Saturday was…unusual for me. You told me in the bar that you weren't following my rules, but the thing was I wasn't either. And I didn't like that. I *don't* like it, really.' He swallowed. His hands were shoved into the pockets of his jeans. 'So I'm sorry I didn't call or text yesterday. I was still panicking.'

She nodded. 'Okay.'

'The thing is, I decided on my cab ride home on Saturday that I needed to slow things down—put some space between us. By last night I'd decided that the best possible thing to do was to end this. Immediately.'

April's stomach dropped, leaving her empty inside. It turned out she *hadn't* been prepared for this possibility. Not at all.

The kettle was bubbling loudly now, steam billowing from its spout. Suddenly, though, Hugh had skirted the counter and was standing right beside her.

'But that would've been idiotic,' he said.

April continued to study the teabags, not ready to risk Hugh seeing what she could guess would be revealed in her eyes.

'And besides, I realised it was impossible the moment I received your text. I'd been kidding myself. I don't want to end this.'

'Okay,' April said again.

She did meet his gaze now, and tried to work out what he was thinking. What exactly did he mean?

His expression wasn't quite unreadable. But equally it told her little. Not like when they'd walked along the Thames. Or even at other little moments scattered throughout that Saturday as she'd told him more about her relationship with Evan, or just before they'd kissed in the centre of that crowded bar.

'Same deal, though? No relationship?'

Deliberately she'd phrased her question lightly. As if that was what she wanted, too.

Wasn't it?

'Of course,' Hugh said.

Then, before she could attempt to read anything more into his gaze or his words, he kissed her.

Softly at first, and then harder, until he lifted her off her feet to sit her on the bench. Then the kiss was something else altogether...it had intent. It was a promise of so much more.

But, wrenching her mouth away from his, April said breathlessly, 'I have to work, Hugh.'

And when he might have told her that it didn't matter, that he was her boss, he seemed to realise he shouldn't say any of that, and that it was critically important to her that he didn't.

She *was* supposed to be working. And for a woman who'd never worked a proper day in her life until recently, it was probably strange that she found that so important. But she did. Working for a living wasn't just some rich girl's fancy to April—it was real... it was her life.

She slid off the counter and walked Hugh to the front door. She stood on tiptoes and kissed him softly, sliding her hand along his jaw. His sexy stubble was back, and she loved the way it rasped beneath her fingertips.

'See you later,' she said.

And she knew she would.

CHAPTER TWELVE

THE REST OF the week was torture.

Delicious torture, but torture nonetheless.

Despite Hugh's best efforts, April was determined to be the most diligent of workers. He thought he understood—possibly—why she felt that way. While the fact that he was technically her boss was mostly irrelevant to him, April clearly felt differently. Which was admirable, really, but also…frustrating.

By Monday afternoon April had quite a collection of things in the 'Hugh' box, having hit a bit of a mother lode of potentially sentimental items in the corner of the almost completed first bedroom.

Most of it was school stuff: finger paintings, honour certificates, ribbons from school athletics competitions. Plus yet more photos—these in battered albums, and mostly of his mother as a child.

The finger paintings went to recycling, and the ribbons to the bin. One certificate in particular he kept—he remembered how, aged about eight, he'd run his thumb over the embossed gold sticker in the bottom right-hand corner with pride. The rest he chucked. He kept his mother's photo albums.

'Penmanship Award?' April asked, dropping down to kneel beside him.

She'd cleared about ninety per cent of the boxes in the bedroom, so she'd been able to open the heavy curtains. Light streamed into the room, reflecting off hundreds of dust motes floating merrily in midair.

'It was a fiercely contested award,' Hugh explained with mock seriousness. 'But in the end I won with my elegant Qs.'

'Wow!' April said. She was so close their shoulders bumped. She met his gaze, mischief twinkling in her eyes. 'I've always rather admired your Qs myself.'

'Really?' Hugh asked.

He leant closer, so their foreheads just touched. Her grin was contagious, and he found himself smiling at her like a loon.

'Yeah…' April breathed.

A beat before he kissed her, Hugh whispered, 'When have you seen my Qs?'

'Oh,' April said, 'I have a remarkable imagination.'

Hugh's eyes slid shut. 'Trust me,' he said, his words rough, 'I do too.'

Minutes later, with her lips plump from his kisses

and her shirt just slightly askew, April slid from Hugh's lap and stood.

'Looks like the 'Hugh' box is sorted for the day,' she said.

'So I'm dismissed?' he said.

She shrugged, but smiled. 'Something like that. See you tomorrow.'

On Tuesday he brought lunch.

They sat on the staircase, brown paper bags torn open on their laps to catch the crumbs from crusty rolls laden with cheese, smoked meats and marinated vegetables.

'Tell me about where you live in Australia,' he asked.

And so April spoke of growing up beside a river with black swans, of camping in the Pilbara and swimming in the rock pools at Karijini. She spoke of where she lived now: in a house where she could walk to the beach—a beach with white sand that stretched for kilometres, dotted with surfers and swimmers and the occasional distant freighter.

'So why come here?' he asked.

Today it was raining, with a dreary steady mist.

'Because,' she said as she wiped her fingers with a paper napkin, 'London was far away. From Evan and my life. And it was different. I imagined a place busy where Perth was slow; and cool where Perth was hot. Perth is isolated geographically—here the world is barely hours away. I needed a change, and I needed it to be dramatic.'

She neatly rolled up her paper bag, being sure that the crumbs remained contained.

'Although,' she continued, 'I imagined walking into my dream job—which, of course, didn't happen.'

'Why not?'

She rolled her eyes. 'Because generally environmental consulting firms want experience, not just a thirty-something with a degree from a decade ago.'

'Why didn't you use your degree?' Hugh asked, confused. 'If that was your dream job?'

'Because...' she began, then paused. She started folding her rolled-up paper bag into itself, her gaze focused on her task. 'Because I travelled a lot,' she said quickly. 'And maybe it wasn't my dream job, after all.'

She stood up and offered her hand for Hugh's paper bag. He handed it to her, and followed her into the kitchen, where she shook the crumbs out into the bin before adding the paper bags to the recycling.

'You okay?' he asked.

She nodded, and then his phone vibrated in his jeans pocket: a reminder he'd set for a meeting he needed to attend.

'I need to go,' he said, and then kissed her, briefly but firmly, on the lips.

'Bye, Hugh,' she said.

On Wednesday Hugh took her to the British Museum.

Initially she'd said no.

'Consider it a team building day,' Hugh said, firmly. 'It's a sanctioned work event, okay?'

She wanted to argue. After all, she'd been playing the professional card hard—and consistently—all week.

'It's great there on a weekday,' Hugh said. 'Not too busy. And it's such a big place that even school groups and tourists don't make it feel crowded.'

Crowds didn't bother her. It was still a no...

'I liked playing tour guide the other day. Let me do it again.'

Oh.

That got her—his reference to their day together... a day she knew he'd both enjoyed and felt uncomfortable about.

Those damn rules. Yet he wanted to do it again.

'Okay,' she said.

On the way, as they sat in the back of another black cab, she wondered—yet again—what exactly she was doing.

She was fully aware that her determined professionalism was something of a cover. Yes, it was important to her to complete the job she'd been hired to do, and to actually *earn* the money that Hugh was paying her. She wasn't going to slack off just because she got to kiss her boss during her tea breaks. Tempting as that was. But also her professionalism was giving her time.

After work she had only a few hours before her job at the supermarket started—and, as their truncated dinner had proved, that wasn't enough time to do much.

It certainly wasn't enough time to do anything more than kiss Hugh. Well, technically it was, but it seemed by unspoken agreement that both she and Hugh were waiting until the weekend before taking things further. When they would have all the time in the world.

The tension this delay was creating was near unbearable. Every touch and every kiss was so weighted with promise that the weekend felt eons away—an impossible goal.

But waiting was good, too. It gave April time to think. To process what was happening.

To process who she was now.

When she'd decided to move to London she'd wanted to discover who she was without Evan. She hadn't worked that out yet, but she did know that she didn't ever want her identity so tied up with a man again.

Not that that was what was happening with Hugh. This thing with Hugh would never be more than what it was—which was fleeting. A fling. And even if it wasn't—even if Hugh *had* wanted more—April knew she couldn't lose herself in 'Hugh and April' the way she had in 'Evan and April'.

Not that it was Evan's fault that had happened. It had been a product of youth and inexperience and an utter lack of independence—and maybe confusing independence with wealth.

It had been *her* fault—*her* error. And she couldn't make it again.

She was different now. As April Spencer she'd proved to herself that she could live alone, and survive without her family's money. Without Evan.

But the way she was around Hugh…that pull she felt towards him…that intensity of attraction and the way it overwhelmed her when he touched her, when he kissed her…

She needed to adjust to this sensation, and she needed time to acknowledge it for what it was: hormones and chemical attraction. Nothing more.

And definitely nothing that she would or could lose herself within.

She would not allow it.

The cab came to a stop beneath a London plane

tree, sparse with leaves in gold and yellow. As Hugh paid the driver April slid out onto the footpath. She stood beside the fence that surrounded the museum—an impressive, elaborate cast-iron barrier—through which she could see tourists milling in the museum forecourt. A brisk breeze fluttered the leaves above her, and April hugged her coat tight around herself.

Then Hugh was in front of her, looking both enthusiastic and just slightly concerned, as if he wasn't sure he'd made the right decision to bring her here.

But April smiled. 'Lead on, tour guide!' she said with a grin.

Hugh smiled right back—with his mouth and with his eyes.

Damn, he was gorgeous.

She definitely hadn't got used to that.

Side by side they entered the forecourt, and as April's gaze was drawn to the mammoth Greek-style columns and the triangular pediment above, she shoved everything else from her mind.

This thing with Hugh—each day with Hugh—was not complicated. It was about fun and attraction. *Only.* She had nothing to worry about.

In that spirit, she grabbed his hand as they were halfway up the steps to the museum's entrance. He stopped, and on tiptoes she kissed him.

'This is fun,' she said. Because it was, and because it was a useful reminder. 'Thank you.'

He grinned and tugged her up the remaining steps. *Yes. Fun and nothing more.*

It ended up being rather a long lunchbreak.

After they'd wandered through artefacts from the Iron Age, and then lingered amongst the Ancient Egyptians, Hugh now stood alone in the Great Court—the centre of the museum—which had a soaring glass roof constructed of thousands of abutted steel triangles. April had darted into the gift shop for postcards for her mother and sisters.

Hugh's phone vibrated in his back pocket, but a quick glance had him sliding it back into his jeans. It was just work, and for once he wasn't making it his priority.

With April no longer by his side it was easier for his brain to prod him with a familiar question: *Why had he brought April here?*

But his answer was simple. Just as April had said on the museum steps: because it was fun. There was no need to overthink it.

He'd wanted to get April out of that dusty, cluttered house and into the London that he loved. He'd been to this museum a hundred times—he loved it here. Even as a teenager he'd come. He'd been attracted to its scope and its space, and to the way people spoke in low voices. Plus, of course, all the exhibitions. It was such a simple pleasure to lose a day discovering relics from a different time and place.

'Can we get a selfie?' April asked, appearing again by his side.

Her bag was slung over her shoulder, and she was digging about within the tan leather for—he assumed—her phone. She retrieved it with a triumphant grin, and he watched as she opened the camera app.

'No,' he said.

'Pardon me?' she asked, her gaze flying to his.

But before he could respond her phone clattered to the floor, finishing near his left foot.

'Dammit,' she said, and crouched to reach it.

But Hugh had already done the same, and now held the phone in his hand. In its fall, the phone had somehow navigated itself to April's photo gallery, and the screen was full of colourful thumbnails: April's hands, shoes that looked vaguely familiar, even a photo of the dinner she'd had with him last week.

'When did you take that?' he asked, pointing at the picture of her meal.

They were both sitting on their heels. April had her hand outstretched for her phone.

'Can I have my phone back, please?' she asked, and her tone was quite sharp.

Hugh met her gaze as he handed it back. 'Of course,' he said.

'Thank you,' she said, her eyes darting to her phone, her fingers tapping on its screen.

He'd only had her phone a few seconds, and it was hardly as if he'd been scrolling through its contents. He'd simply looked at what it was displaying—nothing more. But April seemed uncomfortable, her shoulders hunched and defensive.

'Are you okay?' he asked.

But she ignored him. 'I took it when you went to the bathroom,' she said, answering his original question.

Now she looked up at him and smiled, and the moment of awkwardness passed.

'I wouldn't have picked you as one of those people who takes photos of their food,' he said.

'One of *those* people?' she teased. 'Who are *those*?'

He shrugged. 'You know—the people who feel compelled to document every tedious moment of their existence.'

'Well,' she said, 'sorry to disappoint you, but sometimes I *do* take photos of my food. Or of my shoes, my outfit, or the view, or whatever I'm doing.

Like now.' She grinned, waving her phone. 'So I guess I am one of *those*. *Can* we take that selfie?'

'Hmm…' he said.

She moved closer, bumping his upper arm with her shoulder. 'Come on,' she said. 'They're just photos. They aren't hurting anybody. Why do you care if I or anyone else likes taking photos?'

'I don't,' he said.

'You just disapprove?'

He looked down at her. She was smiling up at him, her face upturned, her hair scraped back neatly from her lovely cheeks.

'No,' he said. 'I just don't get it. Why bother?'

Now it was April's turn to shrug. 'Why not? It's just sharing happy moments with other people, I guess. Or unhappy moments, I suppose.'

A shadow crossed her face—so quickly that he decided he'd imagined it.

'So it's not a narcissistic obsession with self or a compulsive need to elicit praise and garner acceptance from others?' he asked, but he was teasing her now.

'Nope,' April said with a smile. 'It's just sharing a whole heap of photos.'

Sharing.

An echo from their first dinner together seemed to reverberate between them:

I don't feel any urge to share my life with anyone.

'Hugh,' April said, seriously now, 'I want to take a photo of us together. But just for me. I'm not going to post it on social media anywhere. I'm not going to share it with anyone.'

His instinct was still to ask why and to continue to resist. He'd never taken a selfie in his life, and had never intended to.

But he already had his answer. April wanted it for herself.

It was a happy moment she wanted to document.

'Okay,' he said.

He'd surprised her, but then she smiled brilliantly and wrapped one arm around him quickly, holding the phone aloft, as if she was concerned he'd change his mind.

'Smile!' she said, and he did as he was told, looking at the image of April and himself reflected back in the phone's screen.

She took a handful of photos, and then held her phone in front of them both as she scrolled through them. One was the clear winner—they both wore broad smiles, their heads were tilted towards each other, *just* touching. The sun that poured through the glass roof lit their skin with a golden glow, and behind them the staircase that wrapped its way around the circular reading room at the centre of the Great Court served as an identifier for where they were.

'Perfect,' April said.

'Can you send me a copy?' Hugh said, although he'd had absolutely no intention of asking.

April blinked and smiled, looking as surprised as he felt. 'Of course,' she said.

Hugh cleared his throat. 'We'd better go,' he said.

April nodded, and together they left the museum.

On Thursday Hugh didn't come up to the main house.

He sent her a text, just before lunch, explaining that he had back-to-back meetings—something about bug fixes and an upcoming software release.

Not that the details mattered. The key point was that she wasn't going to see him that day.

April set her phone back in place, returned it to the radio station she liked to listen to and got back to her boxes. She was in a new room now—Hugh's mother's, she suspected, but she hadn't asked.

Why doesn't he want to see me today?

April shook her head to banish such a pointless question. He needed to work—that was all. There'd been no expectation that they were to meet each day.

Far from it.

Later that night, after she'd got home from the supermarket, April approved Carly's planned schedule of posts for the following week. Carly had also noted how low they were on blonde-haired April

Molyneux photos, and had asked, gently, if April had made any plans for once they'd run out.

No.

But she knew she needed to.

She was now more than halfway through cleaning out Hugh's house and her credit card debt was nearly paid off. Decisions definitely loomed: What job next? And where? London? Perth? Somewhere else entirely?

And what would she do? Because, as she'd told Hugh, she now knew her heart wasn't in what she'd thought would be a magnificent environmental consulting career.

And what about Hugh?

Again April shook her head, frustrated with herself.

There was no *What about Hugh?*

Hugh was not part of her decision-making, and he was not part of her future.

On Friday Hugh brought lunch again.

Although it grew cold, forgotten on the kitchen counter, as April and Hugh made up for lost time.

Later, Hugh closed his eyes, breathing heavily, his cheek resting against the top of April's head. April, pressed up against the closed pantry door, was taking in long swallows of air, her breath hot against his neck. His hands lay against the luscious skin beneath her shirt...her hands had shoved his T-shirt upwards to explore his back and chest.

'What, exactly,' he managed, his voice gravelly, 'are we waiting for?'

'Time,' April replied, and he sensed her smile. 'Tomorrow.'

He groaned.

'Tomorrow,' she repeated, pushing gently against his chest. 'I need to get back to—'

'Work,' he finished for her. 'I know.'

Finally it was Saturday.

A cab was arriving at three p.m. to collect April.

Hugh was once again playing tour guide—but a mysterious one today, having only hinted at their destination with a dress code: a bit fancy...no jeans.

Another package had arrived from Perth from one of her suppliers: stunning hand-painted silk dresses that would have been perfect if it hadn't been December in London.

So April had spent the morning searching for a more season-appropriate dress along the High Street and at the many vintage clothing shops that Shoreditch had to offer. In the end she'd chosen a mix of modern and vintage—a new dress with a retro feel, in a medium-weight navy blue fabric with a full skirt, short sleeves and a pretty peekaboo neckline.

She'd also bought new stockings and heels, and spent more money than she had in weeks. Although she realised, as she walked out of the store, bags swinging from her fingertips, that this was the first outfit she'd ever bought with money she'd earned herself.

The realisation was both a little embarrassing and also incredibly satisfying.

Right on time, Hugh and his cab arrived.

She rushed to the door with her coat slung over her arm and swung it open.

Hugh was wearing a suit of charcoal-grey and a tie—something she'd never imagined him wearing. He looked *amazing*—his jaw freshly shaven, his hair still just too long and swept back from his face. His eyes were dark, and he was silent as his gaze slid over her from her hair—which she'd curled with her roommate's curling wand—to her red-painted lips, and finally down to her dress and the curves it skimmed.

He stepped forward and kissed her—hard. 'You are stunning,' he said against her ear.

April shivered beneath his touch.

Twenty minutes later they arrived at The Ritz Hotel. The building was beautiful, but imposing, stretching a long way down Piccadilly and up at least five or six storeys.

Inside, Hugh led her into the Palm Court—a room

with soaring ceilings decorated in sumptuous shades of cream and gold. Tables dotted the space, each surrounded by gilded Louis XVI oval-backed chairs, and everywhere April looked there were chandeliers, or mirrors, or flowers, or marble. It was opulent and lavish and utterly frivolous.

'What do you think?' Hugh asked.

'I *love* it,' she said.

Hugh smiled.

They were seated at a corner table. Around them other tables' occupants murmured in conversation to the soundtrack of a string quintet.

'I thought you might like to experience a traditional British afternoon tea,' Hugh said.

A waiter poured them champagne.

'You thought correctly,' April said. 'Although I wouldn't have thought this was really your thing.'

'It's not,' Hugh said. 'So this is a first for me, too.'

'Really?' April said, quite liking the idea that this was new to them both.

Hugh nodded. 'Surprisingly, a reclusive computer science nerd doesn't take himself to afternoon tea at The Ritz.'

April took a sip from her champagne. 'I wouldn't say you're a total recluse,' she said. 'You have to interact with people to run your company, even if not face-to-face. You spend time with me. And with the other women you date.'

Her gaze shifted downwards, to study the clotted-cream-coloured fabric of the tablecloth.

'Selectively reclusive, then,' he said. 'Generally I prefer my own company.'

'So I'm an exception?' April said, unable to stop the words tumbling from her mouth. What was she even *asking*?

'Yes,' he said simply.

But before he could elaborate the three tiers of plates housing their afternoon tea arrived, and the moment was lost. Or at least April decided it was best not to pursue her line of questioning as she didn't like what it revealed. Not so much about Hugh, but about her.

She didn't need to be special, she reminded herself. *This isn't about special. It's about fun. Special is irrelevant.*

Afternoon tea was lovely.

They ate delicate sandwiches that didn't have crusts; scones with raisins and scones without—both with jam and cream, of course—and pretty cakes and pastries with chocolate and lemon and flaky pastry.

They talked easily, as they always seemed to now, in a way that made their first kiss seem so much longer than eight days ago.

Today their conversation veered into travel. April had, of course, done a lot—Hugh very little.

April buried uncomfortable feelings as she deftly edited the stories she told him. She didn't lie, but rather didn't mention details—like the fact that she'd often travelled in the Molyneux private jet, or that her grandfather had once owned his own private island in the Caribbean. Instead she told him only about the experiences: the Staten Island Ferry, the junks in Halong Bay, a cycling tour through the French countryside. Which were the important bits, really, anyway.

She took a long drink of her champagne.

'Why haven't *you* travelled more?' she asked. He'd travelled to the US—Silicon Valley—and that was about it.

'I run my business entirely remotely, so I don't need to interact with people or leave my house,' he said. 'If I did travel the world, wouldn't that seem more surprising?'

April studied Hugh as he drank his champagne. The isolated man he described did not align with the man she'd shared the week with.

'But you love the museum,' she said. 'And that's all about learning and discovering new things. You brought us here today. And you ride your bike. Don't you ever ride somewhere new?'

He nodded. 'Of course I do.'

'So are you *sure* you wouldn't enjoy travelling? You just need to avoid crowds—but that wouldn't be too hard with a bit of planning. There are these amazing villas in Bali...' She paused a split second before she said *where I've stayed.* 'That I've heard of where you have your own private beach. It would be totally private. You'd love it.'

'Would I?' he asked, raising an eyebrow.

'I think so,' April said. 'We could explore the nearby villages and swim in—'

Too late she realised what she'd said, and her cheeks became red-hot. She'd done it again—mistakenly stumbled into a fanciful world where she was special to Hugh—where with her he broke the shackles of the insular world she suspected his mother's hoard had created.

'I mean, *you* could. Of course.'

'Of course,' he said, and when he met her gaze his expression was as frustratingly unreadable as it had been when they'd first met.

The tension between them had shifted from charged to awkward, and April rushed to fix it.

'I can't wait to travel again,' she said, possibly slightly too loudly. 'My credit card is almost paid off, so once I finish working for you I'm going to start saving for my next adventure. I've never been to Cambodia, and I've heard that Angkor Wat is really amazing.' She was talking too quickly. 'Plus, accommodation is really cheap, which is good. And I've heard the food is fantastic. A friend of mine was telling me about Pub Street, which is literally a street full of restaurants and pubs, so you'd probably hate it, but I—'

She talked for a few more minutes, grasping at random remembered anecdotes from her friends and things that she'd read online. She didn't really care what she said—she just wanted to fill the silence.

'So you've got it all sorted?' Hugh asked, and his gaze was piercing now. 'Your plans after you stop working for me?'

'Yes—' she began, and then she took a deep breath. She was sick of all these half-truths. 'No,' she said. 'I have no idea. I have no idea where I'll work or what I'll do. And if I travel—who knows when?—I am as likely to go to Siem Reap as Wollongong or Timbuktu.'

She swallowed, her gaze now as direct as Hugh's. She couldn't tell what he was thinking, but he was studying her with intent.

'In fact,' she continued, 'about all I know right now is that I'm sitting here with you, the hot, charmingly odd British guy I met at work, who is absolutely perfect as my rebound guy. I know that you make me laugh, and I know that you love to show me London as much as I love you showing me.'

She lowered her voice now, leaning closer. Her hand rested on the tablecloth. Hugh's was only inches away.

'And I absolutely know that I *really* like kissing you,' she said. 'I also know exactly where this night is headed. So…um…' Here her bravado faltered, just slightly. 'I'd really like to just focus on the things I know tonight. If that's okay with you?'

Hugh's hand covered hers, his thumb drawing squiggles on her palm.

'Do with this information as you wish,' he said, his voice low, 'but *I* know that I have a key card in my pocket for a suite upstairs.'

His words were so unexpected that April laughed out loud in surprise. But it was perfect. As simple and uncomplicated as their non-relationship was supposed to be. It was what they both wanted—right now and tonight.

Tomorrow, or after she'd finished working with him, or after Hugh had walked out of her life—in fact *anything* in the future—she had absolutely no clue about. But that didn't matter—at least, not right now. As she sat here in this remarkable room, with this remarkable man.

'Let's go,' she said, lacing her fingers with his.

CHAPTER THIRTEEN

IT WAS DARK when Hugh awoke, although a quick check of his phone showed that was due to the heavy brocade curtains rather than the hour. In fact, it was midmorning. Usually by now he'd already be home from his Sunday morning bike ride, showered and about halfway through the newspaper, and probably his second cup of tea.

Right now he had no urge to be doing any of those things.

April lay sleeping beside him, her back to him. His eyes had adjusted to the darkness and now he could see the curve of her shoulder, waist and hip in silhouette beneath the duvet. She was breathing slowly and steadily, fast asleep.

He sat up so he could observe her profile and the way her dark hair cascaded across the pillow. She was beautiful. He'd always thought that, but she seemed particularly so right in this moment.

It was tempting to touch her—to kiss the naked shoulder bared above the sheets and to wake her. But they'd already kept each other awake for most of the night, and she needed her sleep. She was working two jobs, after all.

It had actually been her job stacking supermarket shelves that had inspired him to choose The Ritz. He'd already known he'd need to book a hotel room—April's house was clearly not an option and his definitely was not. A hotel had been the obvious solution for where they'd spend the night together. Clearly he would always have selected somewhere nice. *Very* nice. But The Ritz—The Ritz was a whole other level.

And he'd liked the idea of choosing somewhere so grand and iconic, to give April a London experience she otherwise wouldn't have experienced on a box-emptying, supermarket-shelf-stacking income. Something to remember after all this had ended.

Afternoon tea had been offered by the reservations office when he'd rung to book, and he'd known instantly that April would love the idea. He'd surprised himself by very much enjoying himself too, getting as caught up in the pomp and ceremony as April had.

Hugh's stomach rumbled—a reminder that they'd skipped dinner. Although he certainly hadn't minded the trade-off. He wouldn't have passed on one touch or one sensation for literally anything last night.

It had been nothing like he'd ever experienced.

More than just sex. And, considering sex had always just been sex to him, that was...

Unexpected, Hugh supposed.

Although really had anything that had happened between Hugh and April in the past week or so in any way indicated that when they made love it would be anything but raw and intense and intimate?

No.

He'd told himself as he'd driven in that cab to collect her that tonight would be it: one night with April and then they'd go their separate ways. It would be simpler that way, he'd decided. He'd simply give April his word that he would keep out of her way at work.

But that had been just as big a lie as telling himself that making love to April would just be sex.

April stirred, maybe under the relentless stare of Hugh's attention, and rolled onto her back. But she didn't wake. Now she was just simply closer to him, an outflung hand only centimetres from his hip.

In her sleep, she smiled.

April was always smiling, he'd discovered, and when he was with her he smiled too.

He wanted more than one night.

He needed it.

Hugh had never watched a woman sleep before. His usual protocol was a swift exit the morning after, and he'd always done so with ease. He'd never simply enjoyed lying in bed with a woman, watching her sleep: he'd never felt compelled to.

And *compelled* was the right word when it came to April. In fact since he'd met April so much of what had happened had felt almost inevitable—and certainly impossible to resist.

Not that he was complaining.

But if he wanted another night with April—in fact, many nights—what did that mean?

Did he want a relationship with her?

As he considered that question he waited for the familiar claustrophobic sensation he'd always associated with the concept of relationships: that visceral, suffocating tightening of his throat and the racing of his heart. Similar to the way he felt in pubs, or bustling crowds, or when he was surrounded by his mother's hoard. As if he was trapped.

But it didn't come.

April stirred again, reaching towards him. Her hand hit the bare skin of his belly and then crept upwards, tracing over the muscles of his stomach and chest with deliberate languor.

'Good morning,' she said softly, and he could hear that smile she'd worn in her sleep. 'Please don't tell me we need to check out anytime soon.'

'We have until two p.m.,' he said. 'Hours. But we should probably eat.'

Her hair rustled on her pillow as she shook her

head. 'Later,' she said firmly as she sat up, and then she pushed against his shoulders so he was lying beneath her.

As her hair fell forward over her shoulders to tickle his jaw and she slid her naked body over his he said, 'That works for me.'

'I thought it might,' she said, smiling against his lips.

And then she kissed him in a way that sent all thoughts of anything at all far, far from his mind.

He wanted April. Now, and for more than one night.

The details he'd work out later.

April discovered that walking out onto Piccadilly after checkout, wearing the dress she'd worn the day before and with a biting wind whipping down the street, worked as a seriously effective reality check.

She wrapped her arms around herself, rocking back and forth slightly on her heels.

What now?

Hugh stood beside her. He hadn't shaved today, and she'd already decided that the way he looked right now was her favourite: the perfect amount of stubble, dishevelled hair and bedroom eyes.

They'd left their hotel room for the first time that day when they'd walked to the reception desk to pay. In fact it had been Hugh reaching for his wallet that had been the first fissure in their little 'April and Hugh' bubble of lust.

'Oh—' she'd said, with no idea what she'd actually planned to say next.

He'd looked at her reassuringly: *he had this*. Which of course he did—he was wealthy. A billionaire.

But she wasn't used to a man paying for her. Yes, Hugh had bought her dinner and lunch before, but April had bought him breakfast, and had insisted on paying for their lunch at the British Museum. It had felt as if they were equals.

It was just that she knew how much hotels like this cost per night—she'd stayed at many of them. Not The Ritz, for which she was immensely grateful— she couldn't have stomached pretending if she had. And she'd paid for many of those rooms. With Molyneux money, of course, not her own. Evan had never paid—it would have been crazy. His income was a mere drop within the Molyneux Mining money ocean.

For the first time she wondered if that had been problematic for Evan. Maybe it had? She'd refused to let him pay whenever he'd tried...

Well, there was her answer.

Anyway, April thought she understood money now. Or at least appreciated it more. So Hugh paying thousands of pounds for a night with her made her in equal parts thrilled and flattered and terribly uncomfortable.

He didn't even know her real name.

But then he'd leant forward and kissed her cheek before murmuring in her ear, 'I had a wonderful time last night.'

And that had been such an understatement—and his lips against her skin such a distraction—that worries about money or her name had just drifted away.

Until she'd been hit by the bracing cold outside.

She turned to Hugh. He was already looking down at her. Was he about to say something?

She could guess what it would be: something to reiterate the insubstantiality of their non-relationship, to re-establish this supposedly uncomplicated thing or fling they were doing or having.

Then later—maybe in a few days—he'd end it. He'd finally wake up to the fact that he was, in fact, doing what he'd so clearly told her he didn't want: he was sharing his life with April.

She mentally braced herself for it, simultaneously telling herself it would be for the best anyway. No point imagining their incredible evening had been anything but sex. Even though it had felt like so much more.

But what would *she* know, anyway? She hadn't even realised that her husband didn't love her any more. She hadn't even realised that he hadn't loved her enough *ever*.

Hugh didn't say anything. He was just looking at her with a gaze that seemed to search her very soul.

'So what happens now?' she blurted out, unable to stand not knowing for a moment longer.

'Well,' he said, 'I thought we might go past your flat so you can pick up a change of clothes. Then, if it's all right with you, we could go and grab some groceries for dinner. At my place.'

That was about the last thing April had expected Hugh to say, and it took her a minute to comprehend it.

Another gust of wind made her shiver. She saw Hugh reach towards her—as if to somehow protect her from the cold—but then he stopped and his hand fell back against his side.

Her gaze went to his. He was studying her carefully. Waiting.

It hadn't, she realised, been a throwaway casual invitation.

While she might not know, or *want* to know, exactly how his rule-defined dating worked with other women, she knew absolutely that what he was doing now was outside that scope.

How far, she couldn't be sure. But it was far enough that April glimpsed just a hint of vulnerability in his gaze.

He didn't even know her real name.

She needed to tell him.

But as swiftly as she'd considered it Mila's words thrust their way into her brain to override it: *You don't owe him anything.*

'April?' Hugh asked.

She was taking far too long to answer a simple question.

'That sounds great,' she said eventually. She managed a smile. 'So does that mean you're cooking me dinner?'

Hugh's lips quirked as he waved down a cab, but he didn't answer her question. He probably was. Why else would he need groceries for their meal?

You don't owe him anything.

But of course she did.

She owed him her honesty.

But if she told him, this would be over.

They climbed into the back seat of the London cab and immediately Hugh reached for her hand. He drew little circles and shapes on it again, like he had during afternoon tea. And again his touch made her shiver and her blood run hot.

It also made her heart ache.

She needed to tell him.

Just not now.

She wasn't ready to give him up, or to give up how he made her feel.

Not just yet.

* * *

He did make her dinner.

It was nothing fancy—just a stir fry with vegetables, cashews and strips of chicken. But April seemed to like it, which was good, given he hadn't cooked for anyone other than himself since he'd moved out of home. He didn't mind cooking, actually—it was a skill he'd learnt by necessity when his mother had been at particularly low points, and had been cultivated when his curiosity for varied cuisine had been hampered by his reluctance to socialise much or to have takeaway delivered to his home.

But, anyway, it hadn't really been about cooking the meal, had it? It had been about inviting April into his home. To sleep over, no less.

Not that April was aware of the significance.

After dinner, she asked for a tour of his flat.

As he opened each bedroom door he felt that familiar tension—as if he was worried that behind the door would be a hoard he'd somehow forgotten about.

Of course each room was spotlessly tidy.

April didn't comment on his severe minimalism: there was nothing on the walls, there were no photo frames or shelves...no trinkets. Had she guessed why?

Probably. It wasn't too difficult to work out why the child of a compulsive hoarder might loathe anything hinting at clutter.

The last room he showed her was his bedroom.

Right at the rear of his flat, it had French doors that led into a small garden courtyard, although currently pale grey curtains covered them. The room wasn't large, but there was ample space around his bed, and a narrow door led to the en-suite bathroom.

It was as unexciting as every other room he'd shown her, with nothing personal or special about it. But still…bringing April into *this* room felt different. More than the anxiety he'd felt at each door. Those moments had passed. *This* sensation persisted.

This room—generic as it might be—was unquestionably his private space. He wanted April here—he knew that. But it was still difficult for him. He'd been so intensely private for so long that to be showing April his house and his room—it was a big deal. He felt exposed. He felt vulnerable.

Again he wondered if April realised how he was feeling. She'd walked a few steps into the room and now turned to face him. She'd changed at her place, and now wore jeans, a T-shirt and an oversized cardigan. Her hair was still loose, though, all tumbling and wild. He could see something like concern in her gaze.

'Hugh—' she began.

But he crossed the space between them, and silenced her with a kiss. He didn't want questions or concern or worry right now: hers *or* his. April was here, in his bedroom. And he was kissing her.

That was all that mattered.

CHAPTER FOURTEEN

APRIL WOKE UP before Hugh on Monday morning.

He lay flat on his back, one arm on his pillow, hooked above his head. The other rested on his chest, occasionally shifting against his lovely pectoral muscles as he slept.

She should have told him.

On Piccadilly...outside The Ritz. Or probably the first time he'd kissed her, actually. Definitely last night, when he'd walked her into this room and she'd suddenly realised what a massive deal it was to Hugh. It had been written all over his face: a mix of determination and alarm and hope that had made it clear that *this* was most definitely not in the scope of his non-relationship rules.

But he'd wanted her enough to break his own rules. He'd *trusted* her enough to allow her into the sanctuary of his home. She'd realised, too late, that the young boy who'd never invited his friends over to play had grown up into a man who never had overnight guests. Who never let people into his house or into his life.

It seemed obvious now—from the eccentricity of the confidentiality agreement she'd signed to the way he'd insisted on only email communication when she'd started work—even though he lived only metres away. And his aggravation when she'd turned up at his doorstep in her aborted attempt to resign.

Somehow he'd let her beyond all his barriers—both tangible and otherwise.

Yet she'd been lying to him the whole time.

Hugh was smiling now. He'd woken, caught her staring at him. He captured her hand to tug her towards him, but she didn't move.

Belatedly he seemed to realise she was dressed. His gaze scanned her jeans and shirt, her hair tied up in a loose, long ponytail.

He sat up abruptly. 'What's going on, April?' he asked.

'Do you want to get dressed?' she asked.

It felt wrong that she was clothed while he was naked.

His eyes narrowed. 'No,' he said.

Where did she begin?

'Can I ask you a question?' she asked.

'What's going on, April?' he said again, this time with steel in his tone.

'I just need to know something. Just one thing and then I promise I'll tell you.' She didn't wait for any acknowledgment from Hugh, certain she wouldn't receive it anyway. 'I just want to know the last time you had a woman sleep over.'

He blinked, and his expression was momentarily raw: she'd hit a nerve. That, in itself, was all the answer she needed. But she could practically see him thinking, determining how he would answer her or if he would answer her at all.

Then—heartbreakingly—she realised he'd decided to be honest.

'Never,' he said. 'I've never wanted a woman to sleep over before.'

Hugh wasn't trying to be unreadable now. He'd clearly made a decision to cut through the pretence that had overlaid their relationship. And why wouldn't he? For Hugh, inviting her into his home—and therefore into his life—was the point of no return. He probably felt he now no longer had anything to hide.

And yet she'd been hiding all this time.

'Okay,' she said, struggling to force any words out and hating herself more with every passing second.

'Is that what this is about?' he asked. 'About what we're doing?' His mouth curved upwards. 'I know I've talked about rules and no relationships, but you, April...with you, maybe—'

'Stop, Hugh,' she said. She couldn't bear to hear him say anything like that: words that would tell her she was special and words that she wanted so desperately to be true.

She'd been so caught up in her lies that she hadn't allowed herself to think how she'd feel if Hugh actually *wanted* to be with her. If he had feelings for her. Like she had feelings for *him*.

What feelings?

She shook her head—at Hugh and at herself. None of this mattered because none of it would be an option once she'd told him the truth.

April took a deep breath. 'Hugh,' she said finally, 'I need to tell you something. Something I should've told you at the beginning but thought it was okay not to, I thought it was okay to keep it secret because we weren't actually *in* a relationship, you know? It was just kissing, or sex, or just dinner, or the museum, or afternoon tea... Which, I suppose, when you say them all together, sounds pretty much like a relationship, right?'

Her smile was humourless. But she needed to say this now, because she knew instinctively she wouldn't get to explain later.

Hugh just watched her. He sat there motionless, tension in his jaw and shoulders, but otherwise perfect and glorious in his nonchalant nakedness—the sheets puddled around his waist, the light from the bedside lamp making his skin glow golden.

He said nothing. Just waited.

She swallowed. 'The name on my passport is April Spencer, but for as long as I can remember I've gone by April Molyneux. I'm the second eldest daughter of Irene Molyneux, and I'm an heiress to the Molyneux Mining fortune.'

Hugh recognised her mother's name—she could see it on his face. Most people did...she was one of the richest people in the world.

'When Evan left me I realised that I've never been truly independent. That I've never been single, never had a real job and that I've never lived off anything but Molyneux money. So I got on a plane with practically nothing and came to London to—'

'To play a patronising, offensive, poor-little-rich-girl game.' He finished the sentence for her.

'Hugh—'

But he ignored her, ticking his words off on his fingers as he spoke. 'Live in a shared house, work on minimum wage and pretend to live in the real world. I get it. Then, once you're tired of living like an actual real person, walk away. Feel fleetingly sorry for all those genuine poor people who don't get that choice as you fly home in your private jet. I'm sure you have one, right?'

'That's not what I'm going to do at all—' she began.

But he wasn't prepared to listen. 'So I was just part of the fantasy? A story to share with all your friends when you got home, along with humorous anecdotes about life in the real world. That was what that selfie was for, right?'

April shook her head vehemently. 'No. I didn't plan any of this,' she said. 'How could I? I never expected to kiss my boss. I certainly never expected this week…then this weekend. Hugh, these past two nights with you—they are like *nothing* I've ever experienced. Please understand that. There was nothing false about that—'

'Except the person I thought you were doesn't exist,' he said.

'Of *course* she does, Hugh. The woman you've been with is *me*, regardless of my surname or my family's money. These past few months I think I've been more me than I ever have in my life. *Especially* with you.'

Now Hugh shook his head. 'I'm *so* pleased I was such a helpful, if unwitting assistant in your journey of self-discovery, April.' His tone was pancake-flat.

He turned from her as he slid out of bed. She watched as he retrieved his boxer shorts and pulled them on, and then his jeans. She probably shouldn't have been watching him, but she couldn't stop herself.

Maybe she'd been secretly desperately hoping that this would somehow all be okay—that he'd brush off the specifics of her past and accept her for the woman she'd been with him.

Yeah, right.

Now she knew for certain. Knew that this was it—this was her last few minutes with Hugh…at least like this. He wasn't going to invite her into his room, and more importantly into his life, ever again.

So she looked. She admired the breadth of his back, the curve of his backside, the muscular thighs and calves honed from thousands of cycled kilometres. When he pulled his T-shirt over his head she admired the way his muscles flexed beneath his skin. And then she closed her eyes as if to capture the memory of a naked Hugh she would never see again.

'Who *are* you, April? What do you *actually* do if you're not a backpacking traveller?'

Her gaze dropped to her fingers. They were tangled in the hem of her untucked shirt, twisting the fabric between them. She still sat on his bed, reluctant to move and take that first physical step towards walking away.

'I…ah—' she began, then stopped her repentant tone. *No.* She was *not* going to apologise for who she was—or who she had been. She didn't know which just yet. 'I have a heavy social media presence,' she said.

Hugh rolled his eyes, but she ignored him.

'I use my public persona as a wealthy jet-setting socialite to gather followers—currently I have just a little over one point two million, although that has dipped a little since I've been here.'

She met his gaze steadily.

'I use my platform to attract suppliers and companies that I respect and admire to offer product placement opportunities in exchange for donations to the Molyneux Foundation, which is a charitable organisation that I founded. Last year the foundation made significant contributions to domestic violence and mental health organisations, and while since I've left Perth I've realised that there is far more that I could be doing, I'm still incredibly proud of what I've achieved so far.'

If Hugh was in any way moved by what she'd said he didn't reveal it.

'I'm not some vacuous socialite. At one stage I was—and I own that. And until recently I had no comprehension of the value of a dollar, or pound, or whatever. But I've learnt a lot and I've changed. I'm never going to take my good fortune or my privileged existence for granted ever again.'

Hugh's hands were shoved into the front pockets of his jeans. If she didn't know him she'd think his pose casual, or indifferent. But she did know him, and she knew that he was anything but calm.

'I've been poor, April,' Hugh said, his voice low

and harsh. 'After my father left we were on bene-
fits, on and off, for most of my childhood. We were
okay…we always had heat and food…but it wasn't
easy for my mum. She struggled—you've seen her
house. *She struggled.* It wasn't a game.'

'It was never my intention to trivialise another's
experiences, Hugh.'

'But you *did*, April. Can't you see that?'

April was getting frustrated now. 'What would
you have preferred? That I continued to live off my
mother's money for the rest of my life?'

'No,' he said, and his tone was different now. Flat
and resigned, as if he'd lost all interest in arguing.
'But I also would've preferred you'd told me your
name.'

It was a fair comment, but even so April couldn't
bite her tongue. 'But why *would* I? You were offering me absolutely nothing, Hugh. A kiss, sex, but
absolutely not a relationship. You may scoff at my
so-called journey of self-discovery, but I needed it.
Desperately. For *me*. Why would I jeopardise that
for a man who couldn't even stomach the idea of
officially dating me? I'm so sorry I lied, Hugh, but
this wasn't just about you.'

'So I'm just collateral damage?'

April slid off the bed, unable to be still any longer.
'No, of course not, Hugh. You are *so* much more.'

'More?' Hugh prompted. 'What does *that* mean?'

April blinked. She hadn't answered her own question what felt like hours earlier: *What feelings?*

'What would I know, Hugh?' she said honestly. 'I've been with one other man before you and I totally got that one wrong. All I know is that for you to invite me into your home, and for me to be telling you my real name, there *must* be more. More than either of us expected.'

She was standing right in front of him now. If they both reached out their hands would touch. But that wouldn't be happening.

'It doesn't matter,' Hugh said. 'Not now.'

'No,' April said. 'I know.'

For a while they both stood together in silence.

Finally April stepped forward. On tiptoes, she pressed a kiss to Hugh's cheek.

'I'm sorry,' she whispered in his ear, just as he'd murmured so intimately to her on so many other occasions. 'But I promise you I meant what I said. I was more *me* with you than I've ever been. In that way I never lied to you.'

Then she collected her packed overnight bag from a side table and headed for the door.

'Just finish up today,' he said, sounding as if it was an afterthought. 'I'll pay you your two weeks' notice. Donate it to the Molyneux Foundation—I don't care. But I don't want to see you again.'

April nodded, but didn't turn around.

Tears stung her eyes. Pain ravaged her heart.

Oh. *Finally* she recognised those feelings.

What they represented. Only they were different this time. Amplified by something she couldn't define, but distinctly new, distinctly *more* than she'd experienced before.

What she was feeling was love.

CHAPTER FIFTEEN

One week later

HUGH SAT DOWN at his desk and set his first tea of the day carefully onto a coaster.

It was raining, and the people walking along the footpath above him were rushing across the wet pavement.

As always, he checked his to-do list, which he'd prepared the night before.

Except—he hadn't.

The notepad instead listed yesterday's tasks. Mostly they were ticked off, but the remainder had definitely not been transcribed into a new list for today. There was a scrawl in the corner which he'd scribbled down during yesterday's late-afternoon conference call...but it was indecipherable now that he'd forgotten its context.

Also, surely he'd received an email about something he needed to action today? He *always* added such tasks to his list. He liked everything to be in one place.

He opened up his email, searching for that half-forgotten message in his inbox. Unusually, the screen was full of emails—many unread. Time had got away from him yesterday, so he spent a few minutes now, filing and then responding to the emails that had been delivered overnight.

Just as he remembered he was supposed to be looking for the email with information about today's action, a little reminder box popped up in the right-hand corner of his screen: he had a conference call in five minutes.

He had a moment of panic as he wondered what was expected of him at this meeting—he was completely unprepared—but then he remembered. It was a pitch for a totally new app concept—something he would need to approve before it could begin formal analysis, research and requirements-gathering.

So he was fine. He hadn't forgotten to prepare because he hadn't needed to.

He took a long, deep breath.

What was wrong with him?

He was all over the place: an impossibility for Hugh Bennell. He was always structured, always organised, always in control.

Except when he wasn't.

Hugh dismissed the errant thought. He *was* in control. He was just…temporarily out of sorts. His mother's house was still half full of her hoard, following the termination of April's employment. The weight that had lifted as he'd watched the hoard being dismantled and exiting the house had returned. Oppressive and persistent.

The termination of April's employment.

As if that was really what had happened.

Again the little reminder box popped up—this one prompting him to enter the meeting. He clicked the 'Join' button and immediately voices filled the air around him as people greeted each other, punctuated by electronic beeps as each attendee entered the virtual meeting room.

As always, everyone in the meeting appeared in a little window to the right of his screen. Some were talking, some had their eyes on their computers, a few were looking at their phones. Of course there was, as usual, a generic grey silhouette labelled 'Hugh Bennell' in place of the live video feed of himself.

He wasn't chairing this meeting, so he sat back as the group was called to order and the agenda introduced. First up was a staff member he didn't recognise: a junior member of the research and development team.

She was young, looked fresh out of uni, with jet-black hair and stylishly thick-rimmed glasses.

She was also nervous.

She was attempting to be confident, but a nervous quiver underscored her words. She was sharing her screen with the group, showcasing mock-ups and statistics along with competitors' offerings that didn't cover the opportunity she suggested *they* could capture. But she was still visible in a smaller window, deliberately glancing to her camera as she spoke, as if she was attempting to make eye contact with the group.

Or with the *rest* of the group. She couldn't meet Hugh's gaze, because black electrical tape still covered his camera lens. But of course *he* was the one she was presenting to. He was the one who had the power to approve or reject her idea. He'd listen to the other heads of department to gather their thoughts, but ultimately it was up to him.

The woman presenting knew that, too.

And she was presenting to a faceless grey blob.

He reached forward and peeled the tape off the camera. A moment later he clicked the little video camera icon that would connect his camera feed to the rest of the meeting.

A second later, the presenter stopped talking.

She was just looking at him, jaw agape.

The rest of the group seemed equally flummoxed.

Hugh shrugged, then smiled. 'I'm nodding as you speak,' he said, 'because you're doing a good job. I thought it would help if you could see that.'

'Yes,' she said, immediately. 'It definitely does. Thank you.'

Then she started talking again, her voice noticeably stronger and more confident.

Later, once he'd approved the new app concept and wrangled his email inbox and to-do list back into order, he headed into the kitchen for another cup of tea.

Why, after so many years, had he turned on his camera?

Why today? And—more importantly—why was he okay about it? It should have felt significant. Or scary, even. After all, he'd been hiding behind that tape for so very long.

Instead it just felt like exactly the right thing to do.

He had nothing to hide. He wasn't about to invite all his staff over to his place for Friday night drinks or anything—ever—but still...

Revealing himself to his team, even in this small way, had to be a good thing. Revealing himself *and* his house.

It felt good, actually. Great, really. As if part of that weight on his shoulders had lifted.

Because nothing had happened. Nothing bad, anyway. Something good, definitely. The vibe of the meeting had shifted with his appearance—there'd been more questions and more discussion. It had felt collaborative, not directive as he'd so often felt in his role.

The risk had been worth it.

Unlike other risks he'd taken recently.

The kettle whistled as it boiled and he left his tea-bag to brew while he headed for the spare room, so he could cross off that forgotten emailed task he'd eventually added to his to-do list. It hadn't even been work-related in the end—it had just been a reminder to check if he still had the original pedals from his mountain bike, as one of the guys from his cycling group needed some.

However, it wasn't the container of bike parts his gaze was drawn to when he opened the cupboard door, but the simple cardboard box that sat, forgotten, on the floor.

The original 'Hugh' box. Complete with two faded photos of him with his mother, a crumpled birthday card, an old film canister and that awful finger-painted bookmark he'd made in nursery.

He picked up the bookmark and turned it over and over aimlessly with his fingers. It was just a bookmark. It wasn't anything special. He didn't remember his mother using it, but she would have—just as she'd used or displayed all of his primitive artwork and sculptures when he was growing up.

The bookmark didn't stand out as special, or different. Or worth keeping, really.

But April had asked the question anyway. Despite his clear directions, despite his prickliness and impatience when it came to the hoard he'd so long refused to deal with. And by asking the question April had confronted him with the hoard. She'd forced him to engage and to make decisions.

She'd sensed that he needed to. That if he sat by passively as the hoard disappeared he would be left with a lifetime of regret.

And she'd been right.

He wouldn't keep everything. He might not even keep the bookmark. But he realised now that he needed to make choices. That he needed to pay attention to his mother's treasures and identify his own.

Because there *were* some there. Reminders and mementos of the mother he'd loved with all his heart. And without April they would have been gone for ever.

He bent down and picked up the box. He carried it back into the kitchen, placing it on the benchtop as he fished the teabag out of his mug. He sat on one of the bar stools, staring at the box, thinking as he drank.

He'd spent the week angry because the one woman he'd ever let into his life didn't actually exist. April Spencer had been a fraud, and no more than a façade for a spoiled, rich, selfish woman who enjoyed playing games with people's lives.

But that wasn't true. That wasn't even close to true.

Yes, she'd lied. And it still hurt that the one woman he'd ever trusted could have treated him that way.

But—as she'd asked him—what other choice had she had?

He'd been up-front with all his rules and regulations, and with his immovable view on relationships. And, given he'd spent so much of his life building up barriers between himself and the world, was it fair to be surprised that April hadn't immediately torn down her own?

He recognised what she was doing with her April Spencer persona now: she was being an authentic, independent version of herself, without the context of her wealth or her family which he realised must colour every interaction in her life.

They weren't so different, really. They were both hiding a version of themselves.

April had been hiding the *old* version of herself— the moneyed, privileged socialite, out of touch with reality. Yet he'd met the *real* April: the woman who'd challenged him, who'd made him laugh, and who had made him want to get out of his house and into the real world just so he could share it with her.

The woman who'd cared enough about a still grieving, complicated stranger to save a child's bookmark when it would have been so much easier to throw it away.

Yes, she'd hidden her old self—but she couldn't have been more honest when it counted.

He, however, had been hiding for a lot longer than April. Hiding in his house, in seclusion, behind self-imposed rules and regulations and the piece of tape obscuring his camera.

He'd been hiding his true self until April came along.

He realised now—too late—that everything important in their relationship remained unchanged despite April's disclosure. April Molyneux or April Spencer—she was still the same woman.

The woman he loved.

He picked up his phone.

The interview had felt as if it would never end.

April sat at a narrow table that looked out over the Heathrow runway, her boots hooked into the footrest of the tall stool she sat upon.

Her impatience wasn't the interviewer's fault, however.

'Thank you,' April said, briskly. 'I look forward to reading it.'

'It' being the glossy magazine that was included in Perth's Saturday newspaper. This was a great opportunity for the Molyneux Foundation—she needed to remember that.

The interviewer thanked her again, and then finally hung up.

Phone still in hand, April rubbed her temples. She

felt about a hundred years old—as if this week, like the interview, would never, ever end.

But of course it would. No matter how hard each day was, inevitably it eventually faded into night and a new day would begin. She'd learnt that when Evan had left her.

She'd learnt it again now that...

She closed her eyes. God, how could she possibly compare *one week* with Hugh to fifteen years with Evan? It shouldn't be possible.

And yet she hurt. Badly.

On that awful Monday she'd been a zombie as she'd finished up as well as she could upstairs, sorting through half-finished boxes, leaving detailed hand-over notes for whoever Hugh hired next.

She hadn't cried then. She'd thought maybe she shouldn't. After all, it had only been a week. Surely it wasn't appropriate to cry after such a short period of time?

April had no idea if there were rules about such things.

But in the end, she *had* cried. Silently, curled up in her single bed under her cheap doona, horrified at the prospect that her roommate would hear her.

Crying hadn't really helped, but she was still glad she had.

The next day—before she'd told her sisters what had happened—she'd gone for a walk. She'd walked to the supermarket where she'd stacked shelves even that very night before and resigned.

Then, outside the shopfront, with the large red-and-blue supermarket logo in the frame, she'd taken a selfie.

And uploaded it to Instagram.

I have so much to tell you! #london #newjob #newhair #newbeginnings

And so she'd taken control of her account, sharing with her million-odd followers over the next forty-eight hours what she'd *really* been doing these past few months.

She'd caught the Tube to take a photo of the glitzy apartment she'd originally rented, she'd printed out all her polite 'we regret to inform you that you weren't our preferred candidate' emails and asked a random person on the street to take her photo as she waved them in the air. She'd shared the balance of her embarrassing credit card debt, and then she'd taken a photo of her scratchy, terrible bedlinen, and shared a recipe for a tomato soup and pasta 'meal' that had helped her spend as little as possible on food.

She'd shared how it had felt to be rejected for so many jobs—how it had felt not to have the red car-pet laid out for her as it had been so often in her life. She'd shared her shame at her lack of understanding in her privileged life, and the satisfaction she had felt from earning her very first pay-cheque.

She'd posted about being lonely—being *alone*—for the first time in her life. About learning how to clean a shower, and discovering muscles she'd thought she never had as she'd stacked supermarket shelves.

And she had apologised for not telling her followers any of this earlier, and written that she hoped they would understand. She had told them that she had needed to do this—had needed to be April without the power of her surname carrying her through her life. That she had needed to do it on her own.

What she hadn't shared was Hugh.

She placed her phone back on the table, belatedly noticing a missed call notification.

Hugh had called her.

The realisation hit her like a lightning bolt.

But why?

He must have called during her hour-long phone interview, but he hadn't left a message.

Should she call him?

She twisted in her seat to check the flight information screen.

There was no time. Her flight was boarding soon—she needed to head for the gate.

As she strode through the terminal she wondered why he would have called. It had been a week since she'd last seen him, and they'd spoken not a word. Why would they? Hugh couldn't have made it any clearer: *I don't want to see you again.*

So why call?

A silly little hopeful part of her imagined he'd changed his mind, but she immediately erased that suggestion.

Hadn't she learnt anything? She'd already worked it out that first night, as she'd wrapped herself in her doona, that it was just like with Evan. Hugh simply hadn't loved or even *wanted* her enough to see beyond her past and her good fortune in being born into one of the wealthiest families in the world. To see who she actually was—the woman she had been with *him*.

She arrived at the gate.

Boarding hadn't yet started, and other passengers filled nearly all the available seats. With surely only a few minutes before boarding, April didn't bother searching for a seat. Instead she opened up Instagram, intending to respond to some of her latest comments. This past week her followers' 'likes' and comments had exploded. It would seem that her riches-to-rags experience had struck a chord. Of course now she needed to harness that engagement and monetise it for the foundation. Hence the interview and—

'April,' said a low, delicious voice behind her.

She spun round, unable to believe her eyes.

'What are you doing here?' April asked Hugh.

He shrugged. 'I needed to talk to you. When you didn't answer your phone I came here. Thanks to that selfie you posted I knew where to find you. Had to buy a ticket I won't use, though, to get to the gate—which was annoying.'

'*You* follow my feed?'

He shook his head. 'No. Not my thing. But it came in useful today.'

April needed a moment to wrap her head around his unexpected appearance. She used that moment simply to look at Hugh. At his still too long dark hair, his at least two-day-old stubble, his hoodie, jeans and sneakers.

He looked as he had nearly every time April had ever seen him.

He also looked utterly gorgeous.

She'd missed him.

'What are you doing here, Hugh?' she asked again, wariness in her tone.

'I'm here,' he said, capturing her gaze, 'to apologise for my behaviour.'

April took a deep breath, attempting to process what he was saying.

Over the PA system, a call was made for all business class passengers to board.

'Is that you?' Hugh asked. 'Because I'll get on that plane if I need to. I can't let you leave like this.'

April shook her head. 'No,' she said. 'I can only afford economy seats on my new income. I've got a few minutes.'

'New income?' he prompted.

'Yes,' she said dismissively. 'I'm Chief Executive Officer of the Molyneux Foundation. It's about time I took it seriously, I figure. Fortunately the board agreed.' She paused. These details didn't matter right now. 'Hugh, what exactly are you apologising for?'

'For overreacting,' he said. 'You may not have told me your name from the start, but now I know you were always the real April with me. I guess—'

His gaze broke away from hers and drifted towards the pale, glossy floor.

'I was upset, of course. I trusted you, and that was a big deal for me. When you told me your real name I felt like that trust was shattered. As if you'd been laughing at me the whole time—as if it had been a game.'

'None of this was ever a game for me,' she said quietly.

Hugh was looking at her again now, searching her face. His lips curved upwards. 'I know,' he said. 'I was the one with the rules—not you.'

He was holding his phone in one hand, and he absently traced its edges with his thumb as he spoke.

'I think maybe,' he said, 'I was looking for a reason to justify my lifelong stance on relationships. I've always hated the idea of being trapped within one, of being controlled by one. My mother's hoarding began after my father left her, and I watched her search for love over and over. But she chose the wrong men and they left. That's when she started keeping everything—surrounding herself with things while she was unable to keep the one thing she desperately wanted. Love.'

He swallowed.

'I didn't want to be like her…to *feel* like her. All that pain…all that disappointment. It was all clutter to me, making life more difficult and more complicated. Without love I was in control of my life. And if I walked away from you then I'd be back in control. I would've been right all along.'

Around them people were beginning to line up for the gate, responding to a call that April hadn't heard, with her focus entirely on the man before her.

'But of course,' Hugh said, 'it turns out I was wrong.'

Finally April smiled. Until now she hadn't dared to believe where this was heading.

'This week I *haven't* been in control. I've been a

right mess, actually. Life hasn't gone back to normal—or if it has it isn't a "normal" that's enough for me any more. Not even close. Not without you.'

April closed her eyes.

'April, I want to share my life with you.'

Her eyes popped open and for a minute they stood in silence. Around them the terminal bustled. A small child dragging a bright yellow suitcase bumped into Hugh as he hurried past, sending Hugh a furtive glance in apology.

Very late, April realised they were surrounded by a jostling crowd of people.

'Are you okay Hugh?' she asked, suddenly concerned. 'With all these people?'

'Seriously…?' he said. 'I can deal with any crowd when I'm with you.'

But April saw the way he gritted his teeth as the passengers swarmed around them.

'Nice try, Hugh,' she said, grabbing his hand. 'Very romantic. But we're in the way, anyway.'

She tugged him several metres away, so they stood before the floor-to-ceiling windows that looked out onto the runway. The plane that would take April home to Perth sat waiting patiently.

'April?' he said.

She readjusted her handbag on her shoulder, trying to work out what to say. Joy was bubbling up inside her now, and she was desperate to launch herself into Hugh's arms. But instead she dropped his hand.

'April?' he prompted again, raw emotion in his eyes.

'I want to share my life with you, too, Hugh,' she said. A beat passed. 'I think.'

'You *think*?'

April nodded. 'In fact,' she said, 'I'm pretty sure I'm falling in love with you. But the thing is how can I be sure? We were together little more than a week.'

'*I'm* sure,' he said, with no hesitation.

He loves me, April realised—and that realisation almost derailed her resolve.

He meant it too. It was obvious in the way he was looking at her—as if right now nobody else in the world existed.

It was an intoxicating sensation.

'I'm not,' she said firmly. 'And I want *so* badly to believe that you are, but I won't allow myself to. Not yet.'

She registered, absently, the final call for her flight.

'I was with one man for fifteen years, Hugh. I loved him and I thought he loved me. But I was wrong. Love is...complicated for me right now. I really don't know what I'm doing, and I definitely don't trust my judgement. I think I need time to work that out—to be just April for a while, and make sure that I'm not leaping from one relationship to another simply because being in a relationship is what I'm familiar with.'

To Hugh's credit, he seemed to take no offence at that.

'So you just need time?' he said. His gaze was determined.

Ah, April realised. He was confident—not offended.

She smiled.

'Yes,' she said. She searched her brain for a time frame—for a number that felt right to her. 'Six months.'

He nodded immediately, and April would have loved him a little more just for that—if she'd been allowing love to enter the equation, of course.

'Okay. I can work with that. Gives me enough time to sort out the house and work out any logistical issues.'

April's eyes widened. 'Logistical issues?'

He grinned. 'So I'm ready to move, should you decide you still want me. You know I like to be prepared.'

'You do,' she said, and she was smiling now.

'Are there any rules and regulations?' he asked, teasing her, but he was serious too.

God, there was so much of Hugh in that moment—his rigidity and sense of fun intersecting.

'Of course,' April said. 'Loads. I'll work them out and email them to you.'

She knew he'd like that.

'A question,' he said, as they both heard April's name being called over the PA and both flatly ignored it. 'Are there rules about kissing?'

'Most definitely,' April said, 'but they don't start until I get on that plane.'

And just like that he was kissing her. Her arms were tight behind his neck…his arms were an iron band around her body. It was a kiss that told of their week apart, of mistakes and regrets and hope and…

Hugh broke their mouths apart to trail tiny kisses along her jaw to her ear.

'I *know* I love you, April,' he said, his words hot and husky and heartfelt.

I love you too, April thought. But she wasn't even close to ready to say the words.

Instead she kissed him again.

Then, when she heard her name being called one last time, she said goodbye.

EPILOGUE

One year later

APRIL'S BARE TOES mingled with the coarse beach sand, and she felt the January sun hot against her skin.

Before her stood her sister Mila and her partner, Seb. Mila's *husband*, Seb, actually—as of about thirty seconds ago. Her sister wore a bright red dress and the most beautiful smile as she stared up at the man April knew Mila had loved for most of her life.

The sun just touched the edge of the blue horizon as the small group watched the celebrant say a final few words. The beach was otherwise deserted—the small, isolated cove surrounded by towering limestone cliffs, and with oversized granite rocks interrupting the white-tipped waves.

It was a tiny wedding: just Mila and Seb; Seb's parents; Irene Molyneux; Ivy and her husband, Angus; and their son, Nate.

And April and Hugh.

Hugh wrapped his arm around April and kissed

her temple. She could feel his lips curve into a smile against her skin.

The ceremony over, the group headed for picnic blankets laden with hors d'oeuvres and bottles of champagne. Candlelit lanterns dotted the space, waiting for dusk and the opportunity to flicker in the dark.

April hung back and looked up at Hugh as the sun continued to descend beyond them.

The last beach wedding she'd attended had been her own—to Evan. It had been in Bali, with hundreds of guests—so very different from the wedding they were attending today.

But still today had triggered memories.

Not of Evan, but of how she'd felt that day. Her joy and anticipation at marrying Evan. And her love for him.

She *had* loved her ex-husband. On that day on that beach in Nusa Dua she had thought it impossible to love anybody more.

But she'd been wrong.

And on that night in London a year ago, at Heathrow Airport, she'd found it impossible to trust her judgement when it came to love. After months of berating herself for not realising that her husband hadn't loved her, love had seemed to her like a complex, complicated and impossible concept. A concept she hadn't yet been equipped to handle.

And she'd been right. She had needed those six months. To heal after the end of her marriage. To establish herself in her new role at the Molyneux Foundation. And to live independently of both any man and of her fortune.

She'd also needed the time to work through what she'd learnt while she'd lived in London about her life of excessive privilege and her ignorance of the reality of the world—despite all the charity events her socialite self had attended.

Really, it had taken those six months to love *herself* again. To be proud of what she'd achieved and continued to achieve at the Molyneux Foundation. To let go of the shame of her years of excess.

And to forgive herself for loving a man for fifteen years when he hadn't loved her the same way.

Because she'd realised that love existed even if it wasn't returned. Her love for Evan had been valid, regardless of his feelings. And that love would remain important and special—a love she couldn't regret.

She'd also realised that love grown over a week could be even more powerful than love cultivated over half a lifetime. And that she *could* trust in that love. That she could believe in it and that it could be real and true.

Her rules and regulations for Hugh regarding

those six months had been simple: there was to be no contact.

None at all.

It had been hard, and it had felt impossible, but it had been necessary.

Her week-old love for Hugh had been just as strong—stronger, actually—after all that time, when she'd woken on the morning of her six-month deadline to an email from Hugh.

He was in Perth, and he would be having all-day breakfast at a café on Cottesloe Beach at lunchtime that day. He would love her to join him. If not he would continue his Australian holiday alone, and wish her well.

And so she'd taken herself and her love for Hugh to breakfast.

And his love had been waiting for her. No pressure, no expectations.

'I love you,' April said now, on this beach, as the setting sun painted the sky in reds and purples.

'I love you too,' Hugh said, and kissed her again.

When they broke apart his gaze darted to the rapidly setting sun.

'You'd better hurry with that photo,' he pointed out. 'The light is about to go.'

April grinned. Hugh might not participate in any of her photos, but she now had his full support and understanding of the business of social media.

Today she wore black South Sea pearl drop earrings, and a generous donation from the company
that made them was awaiting after a suitably glamorous photo.

She fished her phone out of her clutch and handed
it to Hugh. A sea-breeze made the silk of her dress
cling to her belly and her legs, and she fiddled with
the fabric as she planned her pose. She needed to
be careful—

But then Hugh was standing beside her again,
holding the phone aloft to take a selfie of them both.

'Hugh…?' she asked, confused.

He grinned. 'I figure a close-up might be easier.
That wind doesn't seem to realise you've got a bump
to hide.'

Only for a few more weeks. And at the moment
her followers were more likely to think her a bit
plumper than usual, not pregnant, but even so…

'But with you?'

Another smile. 'It's about time I become more
than the "mysterious new boyfriend" people are
talking about, don't you think?'

'Are you sure?'

He nodded. 'I've got nothing to hide, April. Not
since I've met you.'

And so, as the sun made the ocean glitter and the
breeze cooled their summer-warm skin, Hugh took
the photo. A photo of the two of them on a beach—

and of the earrings, of course—but mostly of their love. For each other and for the baby they'd created together.

It was a love that April knew was more real than any love she'd ever experienced. A love for the man she loved more than she'd thought possible, and a love for her that had taught her she would always be enough—and more—for the man she loved.

Later, after the sun had set and they were sitting together on the beach in the candlelight, April posted the photo to her followers.

There's someone I'd like you to meet... #love #romance #happilyeverafter

* * * * *

If you really enjoyed this story, check out
THE BILLIONAIRE FROM HER PAST
by Leah Ashton. Available now!

If you're looking forward to another romance
featuring a billionaire hero then you'll love
THEIR BABY SURPRISE by Katrina Cudmore.

MILLS & BOON®
Large Print – October 2017

Sold for the Greek's Heir
Lynne Graham

The Prince's Captive Virgin
Maisey Yates

The Secret Sanchez Heir
Cathy Williams

The Prince's Nine-Month Scandal
Caitlin Crews

Her Sinful Secret
Jane Porter

The Drakon Baby Bargain
Tara Pammi

Xenakis's Convenient Bride
Dani Collins

Her Pregnancy Bombshell
Liz Fielding

Married for His Secret Heir
Jennifer Faye

Behind the Billionaire's Guarded Heart
Leah Ashton

A Marriage Worth Saving
Therese Beharrie

MILLS & BOON®
Large Print – November 2017

The Pregnant Kavakos Bride
Sharon Kendrick

The Billionaire's Secret Princess
Caitlin Crews

Sicilian's Baby of Shame
Carol Marinelli

The Secret Kept from the Greek
Susan Stephens

A Ring to Secure His Crown
Kim Lawrence

Wedding Night with Her Enemy
Melanie Milburne

Salazar's One-Night Heir
Jennifer Hayward

The Mysterious Italian Houseguest
Scarlet Wilson

Bound to Her Greek Billionaire
Rebecca Winters

Their Baby Surprise
Katrina Cudmore

The Marriage of Inconvenience
Nina Singh